ORNAMENT OF LOVE AND THE SEARCH FOR LIFE

Nityanand Sharma

ORNAMENT OF LOVE AND THE SEARCH FOR LIFE

www.usapublishinghub.com
Published by: USA Publishing Hub
Printed In United States of America

PROLOGUE

Crimson dust swirled on the Martian wind, a silent dance across the desolate expanse. Across the velvet sky, the jagged stone of Phobos cast long, skeletal shadows. A lone rover, its solar panels catching the weak rays of the distant sun, trundled across the craggy terrain, its sensors humming a lonely tune.

For decades, humanity had gazed upon this red jewel, dreaming of a second home, a sanctuary among the stars. But Mars held its secrets close; beneath the barren surface and within its ancient canyons lay a truth that had waited millennia to be unearthed.

Pioneers of Martian exploration had spent their lives searching for answers, convinced that more than dust and rock lay hidden beneath the surface. They felt the echo of whispsers, tales of a life and civilization that once bloomed and died under a long-lost sun.

Now, those echoes resonated once more. Nicholas and his brilliant colleague, Susan, felt their pull, while on the northern polar region of Mars, within their research habitat, Dexter and Astral detected a hidden signal, a coded message pulsing through the static. It was there, amidst the red dust and the silent hum of machines, that the story began.

TABLE OF CONTENTS

CHAPTER 1

FAST APPROACH

After graduating from high school in his small town, Nicholas Robertson moved to a bustling city to pursue his passion for cosmology at the university level. He initially resided in a university residence, paying for room and board for two years. Seeking a more home-like environment, Nicholas decided to rent a room in a family home, opting for a situation that included meals. He successfully found a suitable family with reasonable rates for both room and board. Peter and Maggie Smith proved to be ideal hosts, welcoming Nicholas as part of their family. The Smiths also had two university-attending children: Bob and Susan. Susan, particularly, was studying virology with the aspiration of working at a local virology lab.

"During their daily bus commutes to and from the university, Nicholas and Susan gradually grew closer, sharing personal anecdotes and deepening their connection. As they exited the bus, they both headed home. Nicholas, residing on the second floor with a small balcony overlooking the front of the house, hurried ahead. Susan, eager to avoid lagging behind, also made a quick dash upstairs. Their haste led to a brief, humorous encounter on the first two stairs, where they nearly collided."

Nicholas swept Susan into a passionate kiss. Though initially surprised, Susan responded with equal sweetness. His gaze fixed on her face, Nicholas murmured, "You're so sweet; I could kiss you forever." Susan, slightly breathless, replied, "What was that about? You didn't even let me get upstairs!" A smile played on Nicholas's lips as he said, "You're utterly irresistible; your beauty is a precious gift to our love."

Instead of retiring to their rooms, Susan and Nicholas ascended the stairs and stepped onto the balcony. The city lights twinkled below. "How about a trip to the beach?" Nicholas suggested, gesturing in the direction of the coast, just four kilometers away. "Your parents' cottage would be perfect for a weekend." Susan's eyes lit up. "That's a great idea! I'll ask them today."

Susan's parents agreed, and she and Nicholas arrived at the cottage Saturday morning for the weekend. Nicholas immediately set up two loungers on the deck facing the lake. Across the water, low hills covered in lush greenery created a stunning view. Admiring the scenery and Susan's company, Nicholas said, "This is the first time I've been surrounded by such beauty—one beside me and one before me. Susan, I'm so grateful we'll be spending more time together."

Nicholas pulled Susan closer, taking her hand. "Do you think your parents would approve of us spending our lives together?" he asked. Susan replied that her mother had already given her blessing. "So, any plans for our future are up to us now," she added. Overjoyed, Nicholas looked at the hills, then at Susan, and then at the lake.

CHAPTER 2

DIALOGUE

"Susan," he said, "your assurance gives me new life. I want to talk about engagement plans soon. I'm getting so many ideas just being here with you." Susan smiled. "Let's enjoy this moment first. We have plenty of time to make plans."

"Alright," Nicholas conceded. "But I was going to say something interesting about human nature." "Uh-uh," Susan playfully interrupted. "No serious talk. We're here for a weekend escape. We have all week for deep discussions—we practically see each other every day at work. Offices so close, lunches, coffee breaks... you know the drill. Just tell me what you love about being out here." She paused, then added, "For me, it's the beautiful scenery, all that green, the soft breeze, and the gentle lapping of the waves. I've jumped the gun and told you mine already. Now it's your turn." Nicholas chuckled. "You're certainly good at explaining yourself."

"You're right, I'm quite good at that," Susan said with a smile. "But what I really need right now is a cup of coffee in my lounge." She gestured towards the house. "Could you be a dear and make some? We can think about lunch later—it's almost eleven. I think I'll be in the mood for deeper conversations—engagement plans, human nature—after we've eaten." Nicholas grinned. "So that's the secret! No deep thoughts on an empty stomach. I understand. Coffee it is. We can enjoy the view and chat at the same time." He went inside and returned moments later with two steaming mugs.

Susan accepted her mug with a delighted smile, and Nicholas settled beside her. The warmth of the coffee felt good in their hands.

"This is perfect," Susan sighed contentedly. "Nothing beats a hot coffee on a day like this and in my own lounge. Thank you, Nicholas." "Anything for you, Susan," he responded, his gaze meeting hers. Susan's smile deepened. "You're truly the kindest person I've ever met, Nicholas. This afternoon is going to be wonderful. I brought some premium turkey slices for lunch, and I'll whip up some soup and sandwiches later. For now, let's just soak in this beautiful view."

They sat hand in hand, sipping their coffee and gazing at the hills across the lake. "Those hills are so beautiful," Nicholas remarked. "We love them, and that love makes the scenery even more special." "I'm not sure what you mean," Susan replied. "I know," Nicholas said with a smile. "I promised no deep thoughts before lunch."

Before them, the lake's surface shimmered with gentle ripples, like delicate brush strokes on a canvas. A light breeze danced across the water, creating shifting patterns of light and shadow, revealing the fleeting trails of insects skimming the surface and the subtle movements of fish below. The gentle lapping of the waves against the shore was a soothing melody, both relaxing and invigorating.

Across the lake, the hills rose in a vibrant tapestry of green. A thick carpet of grass and trees seemed to glow in the sunlight, the gently rolling landscape creating a soft and inviting vista. The lake reflected the blue sky and the verdant hills, creating a stunning contrast of colors.

After an hour of enjoying this tranquil escape, Susan glanced at her watch. "It's lunchtime," she announced. "As much as I'm enjoying this peace and quiet, we need to eat." Nicholas readily agreed, and they headed inside the cottage for lunch.

After a satisfying lunch, Nicholas and Susan retreated to the sofa. Susan lay comfortably in Nicholas's embrace, a sense of deep contentment settling over them both. The quiet intimacy was palpable. Breaking the comfortable silence, Susan gently reminded Nicholas of his intention to propose and organize an engagement party once they were home. "Of course," he reassured her, drawing her closer. "I'm looking forward to planning everything with you." They realized they could use this quiet time to finalize the details, allowing them to simply share the good news with the Smiths later. They began discussing their vision for the engagement, working out the finer points.

CHAPTER 3

ARRANGEMENTS, OUTLINED

Susan and Nicholas arrived home, refreshed from their time at the cottage. Peter and Maggie welcomed them with beaming smiles. After a brief stop upstairs, they joined Susan's parents in the living room. Nicholas, taking a deep breath, announced their intention to get engaged. He expressed his wish to propose formally to Susan in the presence of both families and close friends within the next few days. Maggie, who had already been informed of their plans during their cottage trip and had discussed it with Peter, gave her enthusiastic blessing. With everyone's approval, the arrangements for the engagement began to take shape.

Peter and Maggie extended an invitation to Nicholas's parents, James and Anne Robertson, to finalize the engagement plans. The day arrived, and the venue was abuzz with excitement. Friends and family filled the room, eager to celebrate the happy couple. With a heartfelt speech, Nicholas proposed to Susan, slipping a sparkling diamond ring onto her finger. Joy radiated from both Nicholas and Susan, their happiness mirrored in the beaming faces of their families and the enthusiastic cheers of their friends.

Returning to work after their engagement, Nicholas and Susan were energized by the prospect of their shared future. Over coffee, as the barista delivered their usual orders, Susan broached the subject of a career change. A smile spread across Nicholas's face. He had been hoping for this. "What about cosmology?" he suggested. "Imagine working together, exploring the universe side by side." Susan's eyes widened with excitement. It was perfect. She decided to start with a cosmology orientation and then take evening astrophysics courses, allowing her to transition smoothly while keeping her current job. Nicholas was thrilled and fully supported her plan, recognizing its clever practicality.

Just a few days later, Susan threw herself into preparing for her new career path. At the same time, Nicholas finalized arrangements with his supervisor for a two-year research project at the Very Large Telescope in the Atacama Desert, Chile—a detail he had kept secret from Susan. He planned to reveal this exciting development after she'd settled into her evening astrophysics classes. But a growing sense of anticipation made him reconsider; he wanted to share the news with her now.

The next morning, amidst the familiar aroma of coffee at their favorite cafe, Nicholas revealed his plans. With their personalized mugs in hand, he told Susan about the Atacama Desert. Her reaction was everything he had hoped for—a mixture of surprise, delight, and a sense of shared destiny. The idea of working together at such a prestigious location and exploring the mysteries of the universe filled them both with excitement. They decided to embark on a new adventure together, starting with researching the Atacama Desert, a place that held the promise of so much discovery.

Nicholas did some research about the Atacama Desert, which is a place of stark, otherworldly beauty. It's known as the driest non-polar desert on Earth, and this extreme aridity has created a landscape unlike anywhere else. The visual aspects of this Atacama Barren landscape have vast stretches of utterly barren, with no visible vegetation. This creates a sense of immense scale and emptiness, where the sky seems to stretch on forever. The landscape is dominated by sand and rows of salt flats, creating a palette of browns, reds, and greys.

The desert is home to incredible geological formations, including Salt Flats (Salars): These vast, white expanses of salt create surreal landscapes that look like frozen lakes. The most famous is the Salar de Atacama, one of the largest salt flats in the world.

Deep canyons and dry riverbeds carve through the desert, revealing layers of rock and sediment. These canyons are surprisingly colorful, with hues of red, orange, and yellow. While not as extensive as in some other deserts, the Atacama does have areas with sand dunes, creating classic desert landscapes. The Andes Mountains border the Atacama to the east, and snow-capped volcanoes can be seen on the horizon, adding to the dramatic scenery. The Atacama's extraordinary sky, clear dry air, and high altitude make it one of the best places in the world for stargazing. The night sky is incredibly dark, revealing a breathtaking display of stars, planets, and the Milky Way.

The extreme dryness and lack of vegetation contribute to an almost complete silence in many parts of the desert. This can be a profound and almost unsettling experience.

The Atacama experiences extreme temperature variations, with very hot days and very cold nights. The air is dry, and the sun is intense.

One can compare the landscape to the surface of the moon or Mars and describe the salt flats as a "white sea" or a "frozen lake," the canyons as "scars on the earth" or "cathedrals of rock," and the sky as "a velvet blanket studded with diamonds."

"The Atacama Desert stretched, a vast and desolate landscape of rock and sand, under a sky of intense blue."

"The Salar de Atacama shimmers in the distance, a blinding white expanse that seems to merge with the horizon."

"The silence of the desert is profound, broken only by the occasional whisper of the wind."

"At night, the Atacama sky explodes with stars, a breathtaking spectacle of light that seems to stretch on forever."

The unique challenges of working at such a remote location! Cosmologists working on the Extremely Large Telescope (ELT) and other observatories in the Atacama Desert don't live permanently on the mountain itself.

Scientists and engineers typically work in shifts or on a roster system. They spend a period of time (e.g., a week or a few weeks) at the observatory, conducting observations and maintenance, and then return to their home institutions or other accommodations.

The European Southern Observatory (ESO), which operates the ELT and other telescopes in Chile, provides accommodation for its staff at nearby facilities.

The most well-known is the Residencia at Paranal Observatory, which serves as the Very Large Telescope (VLT). A similar facility may be available for ELT staff, possibly even an extension of the existing Residencia.

The closest town to Cerro Arma zones is Antofagasta, a coastal city about a 2-3 hour drive away. Some staff might choose to live in Antofagasta and commute to the observatory for their shifts.

Most cosmologists working at the ELT are affiliated with universities and research institutions around the world. They will travel to Chile for their observing runs and then return to their home institutions to analyze data and continue their research.

The Residencia at Paranal is designed to be an "oasis" for astronomers in the harsh desert environment, providing comfortable living quarters, meals, and recreational facilities. It's not a commercial hotel and is not open to the public. It has been described as a "boarding house on Mars" due to the stark, Mars-like desert surroundings.

So, the cosmologists working at the ELT will likely live in a combination of on-site accommodation (like the Paranal Residencia) during their observing shifts or in nearby towns like Antofagasta for longer stays. Once they finish their assignment, they will go to their home institutions around the world for the majority of their time.

This allows them to conduct their research in one of the best astronomical observing sites in the world while maintaining their connections to the broader scientific community.

The more Nicholas and Susan learned about the observatory and the living arrangements, the more their excitement grew. The two-year lead time suddenly felt less like a wait and more like a peri-od of focused preparation. They shared their vision and timeline with their parents, announcing their intention to marry within the year, solidifying their commitment to this shared endeavor. They began to visualize the sheer scale of their future workplace: the Atacama, a desert stretching a thousand kilometers along the South American coast, a relatively narrow strip of land just 145 kilometers wide in places yet rising to breathtaking altitudes of nearly 5,000 meters.

CHAPTER 4

PREPARATIONS

A shared dream ignited a fire in Nicholas and Susan. Nicholas, already a seasoned explorer of cosmological theories, delved deeper into his research. For Susan, the study of astrophysics was a revelation, a world of wonder that she embraced with fervor. Knowing she had a steeper learning curve, she poured her heart into her studies, driven by the allure of a future filled with discovery. Her dedication became a shining beacon, illuminating her path toward stargazing and planetary exploration. This career change was a vibrant expression of her love for Nicholas, a desire to stand shoulder-to-shoulder with him among the stars. Their impending marriage was a testament to their love, a promise of a life shared in harmony. Their future work at the Extremely Large Telescope, under the vast Atacama sky, would be the ultimate expression of their shared devotion to the universe's grand narrative.

A year passed in what felt like a blink, consumed by their shared pursuit of knowledge. Nicholas and Susan, deeply engrossed in their studies, barely noticed the passage of time. Their families, embracing their union, took charge of the wedding preparations, arranging everything from the venue and catering to the officiant who would unite them. The wedding day arrived, a culmination of their love and a joyous celebration shared with family and friends. As they embarked on their honeymoon, a week of blissful escape, they knew that their next chapter—the journey to the Atacama—lay just a year ahead, a testament to their dedication and shared dreams.

Their chosen resort provided a truly wonderful week filled with joy and relaxation. They almost lost themselves in the moment, momentarily forgetting the work that awaited them. Susan gently brought Nicholas back to reality, acknowledging their parents' incredible generosity in making their lavish wedding possible—the time, the effort, and the financial support. She reminded him that they were now in a position to savor their time together and fully dedicate themselves to their shared ambitions. Nicholas wholeheartedly agreed, expressing deep appreciation for their parents' unwavering support and blessings. The week slipped by pleasantly, and with a touch of reluctance, they began packing for their return home.

Back at work, Nicholas began laying the groundwork for their Atacama assignment. He knew that working at such a remote observatory would present unique challenges, and he immediately sought the guidance of his supervisor. Having celebrated with them at their wedding, his supervisor was especially supportive of their joint endeavor. Their research project was clearly defined: to investigate the influence of planetary energies and to identify potentially life-sustaining planets. The supervisor also facilitated their living arrangements at the Atacama facilities, ensuring a smooth transition for their arrival.

To ensure a smooth transition, Nicholas's supervisor coordinated with the administrator of the renowned Residencia at Paranal Observatory to secure two-week stays for both Nicholas and Susan. He also arranged long-term accommodations for them in the coastal city of Antofagasta, a two- to three-hour drive from their work at Cerro Armazones. All travel logistics were handled, including booking their flights to Santiago and arranging ground transportation to Antofagasta. A comprehensive orientation program was also developed to prepare them for their work at the Atacama facility.

The countdown to their departure for Santiago dwindled to just two months. Susan's hard work had paid off; she had completed her studies with flying colors, a source of immense pride for Nicholas, who knew their combined strengths would make them an unstoppable team. They began the practical task of packing, each item a tangible reminder of the exciting journey ahead. The two months passed quickly, filled with both anticipation and the bittersweet knowledge of leaving loved ones behind. The day of their departure arrived, and the airport was filled with hugs, well wishes, and the promise of staying in touch. After two days of travel, they arrived at Santiago Airport, checked into their hotel, and looked forward to the final leg of their journey to Antofagasta in two days' time.

CHAPTER 5

WELCOME AND GAZING THE HEAVENS

Susan and Nicholas arrived at the Cerro Armazones facility to a warm reception from the chief physicist and his team. The breathtaking location and the promise of what lay ahead amplified their excitement to a fever pitch. They were shown to their workstation, the hub of their upcoming research. But before any formal work could begin, they were drawn to the telescope, eager to experience the Atacama sky firsthand. Their first day became a celebration of the cosmos, spent gazing at the stars, lost in the immensity of space. They also dedicated time to reviewing maps and charts, laying the groundwork for their planetary survey and observation work, which would officially begin the next day.

They embraced their time at the facility with unwavering enthusiasm, immersing themselves in exploration and meticulous documentation, their spirits lifted by the awe-inspiring spectacle of the Atacama sky. "I'm so blessed to be here," Susan whispered, her voice filled with wonder. "Being here with you makes it even more special," Nicholas replied, his eyes reflecting the starlight. "I think I've found my calling," Susan declared, a sense of purpose radiating from her. Nicholas wholeheartedly agreed, sharing her profound connection to their work. Driven by their shared passion, they began compiling a documentary of their journey, weaving together scientific data and breathtaking photographs to capture the essence of their discoveries.

Nicholas and Susan had seen the universe through the lens of the Hubble Space Telescope, but the VLT offered a completely different perspective. The sight of our galaxy, the seven planets, and

Pluto, revealed with such astonishing clarity, filled them with a sense of awe they had never experienced before. The dazzling stars held them spellbound, blurring the lines between day and night, between work and wonder. Meals were forgotten, and sleep was sacrificed, all in pursuit of experiencing the cosmos. After a week of this intense connection with the universe, they settled into a more sustainable rhythm. The staff at the facility understood their initial fascination and welcomed them into the community. They began to participate in social gatherings, recognizing that human connection was also essential to their well-being. Two weeks passed quickly, marked by significant progress on their research, thanks to the support of their supervisor and fellow researchers. Throughout it all, their parents' regular contact provided a constant source of encouragement.

The sheer power and scientific potential of the Atacama facility had a profound effect on Susan and Nicholas, solidifying their commitment to ongoing research there. They envisioned returning many times, drawn back by the unique opportunities the location offered. With unwavering dedication, they began compiling a rich archive of photographs and meticulously annotated maps, determined to share their findings with the global scientific community through their head office. After three months immersed in their work with the VLT, they prepared to return home, carrying with them a wealth of data and inspiration, ready to refine their analysis and bring their documentary to fruition.

After three months immersed in the stark beauty of the Atacama, Nicholas and Susan made the trip to Santiago, taking a few days to unwind and process their incredible experience. They then returned to headquarters, eager to begin the next phase of their project: assembling their meticulously gathered photographs and astronomical data into a compelling documentary. They were also excited to recount their adventures to their parents, friends, and colleagues, eager to share the wonders they had witnessed beneath the Atacama sky.

As the evening ended and they were ready to retire, Susan's excitement to share her VLT observations was palpable. She began to describe the Milky Way, their cosmic home, as a swirling, dynamic spectacle of stars, gas, and dark matter, all held in a gravitational embrace. She spoke of the central bar and the sweeping spiral arms, her voice filled with wonder. The concentration of the galaxy's building blocks—gas, dust, and stars both young and old—within the flat disk had been a sight she would never forget. She conveyed the sheer scale of the galaxy, the impossibility of counting its estimated 400 billion stars, stretching across a spiral bar that spanned up to 180,000 light-years. Nicholas added his own observations, sharing his fascination with the galactic halo, the vast, encompassing sphere of older stars, globular clusters, and the mysterious dark matter. The room was hushed with awe as they shared their experience, creating a shared moment of connection to the vast universe. A few hours later, they all went to sleep, their minds filled with the wonders they had witnessed.

The task ahead was daunting: transforming their extensive research into a captivating documentary. They knew it would take months of focused effort before they could return to the Atacama. Undeterred, Susan and Nicholas began working the very next day, sorting through their meticulously gathered data. The sheer scale of the project was undeniable, but they were confident, knowing they had access to the necessary tools, expertise, and the full support of their supervisor and the entire team at headquarters.

CHAPTER 6

ROMANCE AND OUR GALAXY

Around 8 p.m., after a leisurely dinner, Susan and Nicholas sought the quiet intimacy of the lounge. Nicholas drew her close, whispering a playful invitation in her ear. Susan's eyes sparkled with amusement as she lightly swatted his hand, her agreement clear. They had decided to dedicate the next day to each other, a welcome escape from their demanding work. Tonight, however, was a celebration of their connection. Nicholas had arranged a special evening, complete with delectable food and carefully chosen wine. They began with the celebratory pop of champagne, playfully sharing morsels of caviar while exchanging tender kisses. As the evening unfolded, Nicholas reflected on their time spent beneath the vast expanse of the Atacama sky, how their shared experience of gazing at the stars had deepened their bond and created a profound sense of connection. He expressed the immense joy he felt simply being with her. Susan's laughter was warm and affectionate; she found his hints endearing. They enjoyed their meal and wine, lost in each other's company. Later, within the privacy of their suite, their love deepened, a quiet testament to the powerful connection they shared, and their love found its fullest expression.

They slept in the next morning, enjoying the lingering effects of their relaxing evening. Susan woke first and quietly made her way to the kitchen to prepare a hot breakfast. Nicholas soon followed, greeting her with a warm kiss before brewing coffee. After a satisfying meal, they settled onto the sofa, enjoying the comfortable silence. Nicholas then headed off for a shower, while Susan picked up a magazine and became engrossed in an article about the life force and the natural cycle of growth and decay on Earth. She finished reading before taking her own shower. Feeling thoroughly refreshed, they decided to dedicate the day to conversation and lighthearted activities, knowing that a specific task awaited them the following day.

The breathtaking view of their home galaxy, as revealed by the VLT, remained etched in their minds. Now, the task before them was to transform that cosmic spectacle into a compelling story. They began the process of organizing their photographs and videos, striving to capture the essence of the Milky Way: its central bar of stars, the graceful sweep of its spiral arms, the vibrant glow of young stars alongside the ancient light of globular clusters, and the unseen influence of gas, dust, and dark matter, all swirling within the galaxy's gravitational embrace. They knew this would be a demanding undertaking, requiring careful reflection and creative sequencing to convey the wonders of the Milky Way to a general audience.

The day proved highly productive, though they only managed to organize about ten percent of their extensive photograph collection. Susan, recognizing the scale of the task, skillfully sought assistance from her colleagues. The captivating nature of the material drew everyone in, and they worked together with Nicholas and Susan. The compilation process took nearly six months. They were delighted with the result: a compelling media package ready for release.

Having entrusted their media package to their supervisor, Susan and Nicholas prepared for their second expedition to the Atacama Observatory. This time, their focus was set: the search for exoplanets and signs of extraterrestrial life. Arriving at their familiar spot on Atacama Hill, they settled into their workstation at the VLT. With her usual enthusiasm, Susan adjusted her telescope, its lens trained on the star-studded canvas of the night sky. The cool desert breeze nipped at her cheeks, but the breathtaking panorama of the Milky Way warmed her from within. She waited for Nicholas, knowing he wouldn't be long. He'd arrive with hot coffee, and together they'd soon be lost in the wonder of the cosmos under the observatory dome's dim light. As she sipped her coffee, a shooting star streaked across the heavens, and Susan made a wish—for Nicholas's arrival, his laughter, and the discoveries that awaited them.

Over their coffee, a quiet intimacy settled between them. Nicholas, his heart overflowing with love for Susan, leaned in and kissed her—a kiss that was both passionate and tender. The warmth of the embrace drew her onto his lap, and as they looked up at the star-studded sky, their shared excitement created a magical, almost surreal atmosphere. Looking into Susan's eyes, his voice sincere and full of emotion, Nicholas spoke from the heart. "I'm committed to building my dreams with you, and yours," he said. "I need you, my wife, now more than ever. Under this incredible sky, I want to build our future together." Tears welled in Susan's eyes as she listened, her heart overflowing with the depth of his love.

In the quiet sanctuary of the observatory, Susan and Nicholas surrendered to the intimacy of the moment, their thoughts of careers and ambition receding into the distance. The immensity of the universe served as a backdrop, highlighting the preciousness of their love—a beacon of warmth and connection in the face of cosmic vastness. The stillness deepened their introspection, drawing them into a shared space of vulnerability and understanding. They felt, more strongly than ever, that in this boundless universe, their love was their anchor, a source of profound meaning and belonging. Nicholas, with a tender gesture, offered Susan the thermos of hot chocolate he had thoughtfully brought. The shared warmth of the drink created a moment of quiet contentment, reinforcing the powerful sense that love could make any problem seem insignificant, whether it was the challenges of their research or the awe-inspiring spectacle of meteor showers and swirling galaxies.

"I'm so thrilled we're exploring cosmology together," Nicholas said to Susan, a spark of excitement in his eyes. "I've been captivated by the universe since I was a kid, and now, diving into this research with you... it's incredible." Although Susan's university studies had provided a foundation in cosmology, Nicholas was eager to delve into the finer details, hoping to ignite their shared passion for discovering new stars and exoplanets—perhaps even finding a trace of life.

The research shows us how the universe evolved, and we have to know more about how the Big Bang Theory, black holes, and galaxies are connected, so that we can determine where the building blocks of life are present and how they interact with each other.

The picture of the universe out there, as the research shows, tells us that the Big Bang is the foundation of the prevailing cosmological model for the universe's origin. It states that the universe began as an extremely hot, dense state and has been expanding and cooling ever since. This expansion led to the formation of atoms and, eventually, stars and galaxies.

The Galaxies are the Cosmic Cities. They are vast collections of stars, gas, dust, and dark matter, all held together by gravity. They are the major building blocks of the universe.

Our own Galaxy, the Milky Way, is just one of billions of galaxies in the observable universe.

The Black Holes are the Galactic Anchors, and regions of spacetime with such strong gravity that nothing, not even light, can escape.

Supermassive black holes (SMBHs) reside at the centers of most galaxies, including the Milky Way. These SMBHs play a crucial role in galaxy formation and evolution.

It is believed that in the early universe, shortly after the Big Bang, fluctuations in density led to the formation of both galaxies and black holes.

Galaxy Formation: SMBHs at the centers of galaxies act as "seeds" around which galaxies form and grow. Their gravity pulls in gas and dust, fueling star formation and contributing to the galaxy's overall structure.

Black holes can also influence galaxy evolution through "feedback." As matter falls into a black hole, it can release tremendous amounts of energy in the form of jets and winds. This energy can heat up and push away gas in the galaxy, regulating star formation and preventing galaxies from becoming too massive.

Simply, Imagine the Big Bang as the initial spark that ignited the universe. This led to the formation of galaxies, which are like giant cities of stars. And at the heart of these cities, there are powerful an-chors—supermassive black holes—that help shape and guide the growth of these galactic cities.

Scientists are still actively researching the precise relationship between black holes and galaxies. It's a complex interplay, and there are many unanswered questions. However, it's clear that these three elements are deeply connected and essential to our understanding of the universe's past, present, and future.

We have learned that our human body is made up of some key elements and some conditions that make our body work.

These key elements and conditions that are generally considered essential for life as we know it are CHNOPS, which are the most abundant elements in living organisms on Earth:

C for Carbon, which is the backbone of organic molecules. Its ability to form stable bonds with many other elements, including it-self, allows for the complex structures needed for life.

H for Hydrogen, a component of water and many organic mole-cules.

N for Nitrogen, a key component of amino acids (the building blocks of proteins) and nucleic acids (DNA and RNA).

O for Oxygen, essential for respiration in many organisms and a component of water and many organic molecules.

P for Phosphorus, a crucial component of nucleic acids, ATP (the energy currency of cells), and cell membranes.

S for Sulfur. It's found in some amino acids and proteins, play-ing a role in protein structure and function.

Water (H_2O): is an excellent solvent, meaning it can dissolve many substances. This is crucial for transporting nutrients and re-moving waste within cells and serves as a medium for Reactions, as many biochemical reactions occur in water.

Water also has a high heat capacity, meaning it can absorb a lot of heat without a significant temperature change. This helps regulate temperature within organisms and environments.

Life also requires a source of energy to carry out its functions. This energy can come from various sources, such as Sunlight (Photosynthesis), Plants and some other organisms use sunlight to convert carbon dioxide and water into glucose (sugar) for energy.

Some organisms, particularly in environments without sunlight (like deep-sea vents), obtain energy from chemical compounds.

Life also needs a relatively stable environment to survive, which includes:

Temperature: Temperatures need to be within a range that allows for liquid water and stable organic molecules.

Pressure: Pressure needs to be within a range that allows for stable cell structures.

Radiation: Protection from harmful radiation is important, as it can damage DNA and other biological molecules.

Important Considerations:

As we learned, this is based on our understanding of life on Earth. It's possible that life could exist in other forms with different requirements, but we don't have evidence of that yet.

Habitability: When searching for life beyond Earth, scientists look for these key elements and conditions, which contribute to a planet's "habitability."

In summary, the key elements for life as we know it are CHNOPS, water, an energy source, and a stable environment. These factors are interconnected and play crucial roles in the origin, survival, and evolution of life.

"Imagine," Nicholas said to Susan, "trying to find a tiny flicker of life in the vast darkness of space. That's what we're doing. We're searching for biosignatures – chemical whispers of life – in the atmospheres of distant exoplanets. We analyze the starlight that filters through these atmospheres, looking for telltale signs: unusual combinations of gases like oxygen, methane, and ozone; perhaps even hints of vegetation on the surface, or unique patterns in the light reflected to us. It's like trying to decipher a cosmic code. We're building on the work of so many scientists who have used James Webb and VLT to peer into the secrets of these distant worlds. It's a long shot, but the potential reward – discovering life beyond Earth – is immeasurable." Susan was captivated by Nicholas's description, and he felt a surge of satisfaction in sharing his passion for this groundbreaking research.

"This groundbreaking research is so eye-opening that we should focus solely on new stars," Susan declared to Nicholas. He wholeheartedly agreed, suggesting they dedicate the next two years to exploring only newly discovered exoplanets and their host stars, building upon the insights gleaned from their current findings. Their primary focus would be to meticulously observe and analyze the key elements and conditions that contribute to a planet's potential habitability.

Following their comprehensive data collection, Nicholas and Susan resolved to spend two more years conducting observations at the Atacama VLT facility in various phases. Settling into the lounge with cups of coffee, they began to brainstorm new avenues of research. "I dream of discovering an exoplanet teeming with life, a world as vibrant and diverse as our own Earth," Susan mused. "But," she added with a playful grin, "I'm hoping the inhabitants are a bit more aesthetically pleasing than the typical depictions in popular media – you know, the long-necked, large-eyed creatures with elongated faces." Nicholas chuckled, understanding her playful apprehension.

"I completely agree," Nicholas responded. "I, too, hope that these potential extraterrestrial beings are a peaceful and harmonious society. We witness far too much conflict and warfare on Earth, and I sincerely hope to discover a planet where such destructive tendencies are absent." They shared a wry chuckle. "Of course," Nicholas added, "determining their social and political structure through telescopic observations alone would be quite a challenge."

"I understand that determining their social structure requires further investigation," Susan acknowledged, "but wouldn't it be extraordinary to discover a planet where society transcends the limitations we experience on Earth? A world free from hatred, violence, greed, lust, jealousy, anger, ego, lies, and all the vices that plague us." Nicholas enthusiastically agreed, "Who wouldn't yearn for such a utopia?" Their conversation, charged with a mixture of hope and wonder, continued over their coffee until they finally succumbed to sleep.

After a restful night, Susan and Nick enjoyed a hearty breakfast before heading to their workstation. They began their day by reviewing existing research on Proxima Centauri b, the exoplanet orbiting the red dwarf star Proxima Centauri. While situated within the habitable zone and possessing the potential to support liquid water, the challenges of detecting life on this distant world became abundantly clear. Proxima Centauri b lies 9.46 trillion kilometers from Earth, and even the New Horizons probe, traveling at a remarkable 58,000 kilometers per hour, would require an estimated 80,000 years to reach its destination. This staggering reality left them both feeling a profound sense of awe and a renewed appreciation for the vastness of the universe.

The following morning, Nicholas and Susan decided to take a week-long vacation, escaping the demands of their research to rejuvenate amidst the breathtaking scenery of San Pedro de Atacama. Nestled within an oasis in the heart of the Chilean desert, this renowned tourist destination offered a unique blend of natural wonders, including the awe-inspiring Atacama Salt Flats, geysers, and unparalleled stargazing opportunities. While eager to unwind and soak in the desert atmosphere, they also planned to dedicate some time to reviewing the latest advancements in exoplanet research. During their downtime, they intended to delve into the fascinating techniques employed by scientists in their quest to detect and characterize life beyond our solar system, including Transit Spectroscopy, the Radial Velocity Method, Direct Imaging, the capabilities of Space-Based Telescopes, and the ambitious goal of Interstellar Travel. They planned to revisit these concepts in greater detail upon their return to the observatory.

Returning to the observatory, a renewed sense of purpose and excitement fueled Nicholas and Susan as they eagerly returned to their workstations. They immediately began discussing the various techniques they would employ in their search for extraterrestrial life, acknowledging the immense challenges posed by the vast interstellar distances separating countless stars and planets.

They understood the significance of Transit Spectroscopy, where the filtering of starlight through a planet's atmosphere during a transit can reveal the presence of key biosignatures, such as water vapor, methane, oxygen, and carbon dioxide. The Radial Velocity Method, they recognized, would be crucial in determining the mass and orbital characteristics of exoplanets, providing crucial clues about their habitability.

Furthermore, they anticipated utilizing their powerful telescope for direct imaging of distant exoplanets, allowing for detailed observations of planetary surfaces, atmospheres, and potential signs of life, such as vegetation or liquid water. While acknowledging the long-term nature of interstellar travel, they agreed to focus their immediate efforts on these more accessible and immediate avenues of research.

For the first two months, Susan and Nicholas immersed themselves in their search for extraterrestrial life, diligently employing the techniques they had so meticulously researched. Day and night, they scrutinized galaxies, planets, stars, and even black holes, their minds constantly grappling with the vastness of the universe and the immeasurable number of celestial bodies scattered across its cosmic expanse. Despite their tireless efforts, however, they encountered no conclusive evidence of life beyond Earth.

Their observations conducted using the Very Large Telescope, the James Webb Space Telescope, and the Hubble Telescope, failed to reveal any new exoplanets exhibiting the telltale signs of life—the presence of water vapor, methane, oxygen, and carbon dioxide in their atmospheres. This lack of concrete findings left them feeling a mixture of discouragement and an unwavering fascination with the universe, a universe that continued to inspire awe and wonder despite its apparent silence.

They both decided to go back to their hometown and took a leave of absence from work to focus on their married life. They decided to keep abreast with cosmology and exoplanet research. Their supervisor agreed to allow them to work part-time remotely so that they can go back full-time to their office after two years. They had access to the latest publications of research on cosmology. They went to an island retreat for a few weeks. The island resort was close to their town, which appealed to them to retreat. This break gave them sufficient flexibility to recharge. Every day they were busy with daytime activities, and during the nighttime, they couldn't stop stargazing. During their island retreat, they enjoyed leisurely days exploring the island's natural beauty, indulging in water sports, and evenings spent gazing at the star-studded sky. Nights under the vast expanse of the cosmos became their own personal observatory, fueling their curiosity and rekindling their passion for the universe. Despite the temporary break from their research, they kept abreast of the latest advancements in cosmology, staying connected to the scientific community through online publications and journals. Their supervisor graciously granted them a part-time remote work arrangement, allowing them to maintain a connection to their research while enjoying their well-deserved break. This period of rejuvenation proved invaluable, providing them with the mental and emotional clarity to approach their research with renewed vigor upon their return.

"Every day, Susan and Nicholas would stroll along the beach, their fingers intertwined. They delighted in playful moments—rolling in the white sand, splashing each other in the crystal-clear water, and playfully wrestling each other into the waves. Stolen kisses under the warm sun and whispered secrets shared during quiet moments on the beach deepened their connection. The island itself, with its serene beauty, mirrored their growing intimacy. Evenings, once filled with scientific debates, now echoed with the gentle rhythm of the waves and the soft murmur of their voices as they shared their dreams, their fears, and their hopes for the future, their gazes drawn to the constellations twinkling above.

The next morning, Nicholas surprised Susan with an unexpected display of affection. After breakfast, he pulled her close, enveloping her in a warm embrace. "Today," he declared, "I'm the chef. I'll cook both meals, and we'll spend the afternoon watching movies and dreaming about our future." He sealed his words with a tender kiss, a mischievous glint in his eyes. Susan, taken aback by his unusual enthusiasm, couldn't help but smile. "I like the sound of that," she replied, though a flicker of concern lingered beneath her amusement. Nicholas, usually so immersed in his research, seemed unusually eager to escape the demands of their work and simply enjoy each other's company.

Susan settled comfortably at the dining table, her gaze drawn to the shimmering lake beyond the window. Nicholas, intent on surprising her, insisted she relax while he handled the culinary duties. With a contented sigh, Susan obliged, her attention shifting to the picturesque scene unfolding before her—yachts gliding across the water, the gentle lapping of waves against the shore.

At midday, Nicholas emerged from the kitchen, bearing a platter laden with fragrant spiced rice and a perfectly grilled fish. Susan, captivated by the aroma, couldn't help but praise his culinary efforts, her voice soft with appreciation as she sipped her light beer and gently squeezed his hand.

Later, they settled onto the plush sofa, a romantic comedy streaming on the smart television. Lost in the gentle ebb and flow of the movie, they shared a quiet intimacy, their hands occasionally brushing against each other, their eyes occasionally meeting with a knowing smile.

They were immersed in watching the movie and caressing without noticing that it was already getting dark and the stars were coming out, getting brighter and brighter.

Feeling refreshed, Susan excused herself to freshen up while Nicholas assured her that dinner would be ready soon. He encouraged her to relax and enjoy the afternoon at her own pace. Susan, feeling a pleasant sense of anticipation, decided to indulge in a short nap on the sofa.

When dinner was finally served, Susan, feeling revitalized, was eager to savor the meal Nicholas had prepared. He, in turn, was delighted to see her looking so relaxed and content. They enjoyed a leisurely dinner, accompanied by a bottle of their favorite red wine, savoring each bite and sharing stories of their day.

As they settled into bed later that evening, Nicholas leaned in close, a mischievous glint in his eyes. "I have something to discuss with you," he began, his voice low and intimate. Susan, intrigued by his sudden seriousness, eagerly awaited his revelation.

"Susan," Nicholas began, his voice husky with emotion, "you look absolutely stunning in my arms. We've spent the last few years searching for life on other planets, exploring the vastness of the universe. But here on Earth," he continued, gazing into her eyes, "we have the most beautiful life imaginable." He paused, his expression softening. "So, tell me, what do you think about starting a family of our own? I think our families would be overjoyed to hear the news."

Susan, her eyes wide with surprise and delight, was speechless for a moment. Then, she leaned forward and kissed him passionately, burying her face in his chest. They spent the rest of the night whispering sweet nothings, their laughter mingling with the gentle sounds of the island.

The next morning dawned with a newfound sense of joy and anticipation. As they awoke, a quiet understanding passed between them – their lives were about to embark on a new and exciting chapter.

Susan and Nicholas went on with their daily routine. They also finished the reading assignment they had planned before arriving at the island. One of the items in the assignment was to study about the Mars, noting that it lacks several crucial conditions that are essential for sustaining life as we know it:

Thin Atmosphere: Mars has a very thin atmosphere, composed mostly of carbon dioxide.

Lack of Oxygen: The Martian atmosphere contains almost no oxygen, which is essential for most life on Earth.

Low Atmospheric Pressure: The low atmospheric pressure on Mars makes it difficult for liquid water to exist on the surface.

Extreme Cold: Mars experiences extremely cold temperatures, with average temperatures around -80 degrees Fahrenheit (-60 degrees Celsius).

Large Temperature Fluctuations: Temperatures can fluctuate significantly between day and night due to the thin atmosphere.

High Levels of Radiation: Mars lacks a significant global magnetic field to protect it from harmful solar and cosmic radiation. This radiation can be detrimental to living organisms.

Limited Liquid Water: While evidence suggests that liquid water may have existed on Mars in the past, it is scarce today. Most water on Mars exists as ice in the polar caps and possibly underground.

Lack of Nutrients: Martian soil is generally deficient in the nutrients necessary to support plant life.

These conditions create a harsh and inhospitable environment for most known life.

However, it's important to note that:

Past Habitability: Scientists believe that Mars may have been more habitable in the past, with a thicker atmosphere and liquid water on the surface.

Potential for Life: Some scientists speculate that microbial life may still exist in subsurface environments on Mars, where conditions may be more favorable.

The five most abundant gases in the Martian atmosphere are:

1. Carbon Dioxide (CO_2): This is the dominant gas, making up about 95% of the atmosphere.

2. Nitrogen (N_2): The second most abundant gas, accounting for around 2.7%.

3. Argon (AR): The third most abundant gas, making up about 1.6%.

4.Oxygen (O2): A minor component, present in trace amount.

5.Carbon Monoxide (CO): Also a minor component, present in trace amounts.

The ongoing exploration of Mars by various space agencies is crucial for understanding the planet's past, present, and potential for future habitability.

Knowing the information from NASA, they would conduct research on finding solutions to make conditions habitable on Mars. This involves studying techniques like:

Terraforming: Exploring methods to thicken the Martian atmosphere, such as introducing greenhouse gases to trap heat and raise temperatures.

Creating a Magnetosphere: Investigating ways to establish a magnetic field to protect Mars from harmful solar radiation.

Introducing Earth-based organisms: Researching the feasibility of introducing hardy microorganisms to help terraform the planet by producing oxygen and enriching the soil.

A month passed, and Susan began experiencing morning sickness and fatigue. A visit to the doctor confirmed their suspicions: Susan was pregnant. The news filled their hearts with joy, and their families were overjoyed.

Susan gave birth to a beautiful baby girl, whom they named Sally. With the arrival of their daughter, their research took a backseat. Nicholas and Susan dedicated themselves to caring for their child, knowing that their scientific pursuits could wait. They agreed that they would resume their full-time research after a three-year sabbatical, allowing them to cherish these precious early years with their daughter.

CHAPTER 7

A VISIT

"Nicholas savored the rich, smoky aroma of his Glenlivet single malt, an unusual indulgence for him. He felt a deep sense of contentment, a warmth spreading through him that had nothing to do with the alcohol. In the living room, Susan sat on the sofa, gently rocking their daughter, Sally, in her arms. 'She's the most beautiful thing in the world,' Susan murmured, her voice filled with love.

Nicholas smiled, his heart swelling with a love he never knew existed. 'I know,' he replied, joining them on the sofa. He carefully took Sally from Susan's arms, cradling her in his own. 'My two favorite girls,' he whispered, pressing a gentle kiss to Sally's soft cheek. 'I love you both more than words can say. I wouldn't trade this moment for anything in the world.'

Susan, her eyes shining, leaned into him, and they shared a tender kiss. 'I love you too, Nicholas,' she whispered, 'more than you know.'

As he held his daughter close, Nicholas realized that his life had found a perfect balance. His passion for research, his love for Susan, and the boundless joy of fatherhood—all these elements now intertwined, creating a harmonious symphony of life.

Nicholas stirred beside Susan, a strange excitement buzzing within him. 'Susan,' he whispered, his voice a mixture of wonder and disbelief, 'I had the most extraordinary dream.' He described the encounter: a couple, tall and elegant, with skin that shimmered with an almost luminescent quality, had appeared before him.

'The man,' Nicholas continued, his voice trembling slightly, 'was the most breathtakingly handsome man I've ever seen. At least six and a half feet tall, with skin as pale as moonlight, he spoke in the softest voice, introducing himself as Dexter. His wife, Astral, was equally stunning, her beauty both ethereal and captivating. They claimed to be from Mars, traveling across the cosmos for two centuries to visit a family on Earth.'

Nicholas paused, still awestruck by the vividness of his dream. 'I couldn't believe it,' he confessed. 'I invited them in, completely bewildered by their presence. Their beauty was mesmerizing, otherworldly. Their physiques were perfect; their eyes... they seemed to pierce right through me.'

Susan listened intently, her own imagination ignited by Nicholas's vivid description. "It sounds like an incredible dream, Nicholas," she murmured, pulling him closer. "Perhaps it's a message from the universe, a sign that our search for life beyond Earth may not be in vain."

Nicholas, still lost in the afterglow of his dream, couldn't help but wonder. Could it be a premonition? Or simply the result of a mind steeped in the mysteries of the cosmos?

"Nicholas," his voice trembling with a mixture of disbelief and excitement, told Susan, "Dexter and Astral are coming to visit us next month! They plan to spend six months vacationing on Earth." He explained that they had discovered Nicholas and Susan's research through their own extensive explorations of the universe.

"They believe," Nicholas continued, "that we've been searching for extraterrestrial life in the wrong places. They explained that Mars, our closest neighbor, has been home to a thriving civilization for millions of years. They have an atmosphere like Earth, with abundant oxygen and an ozone layer to sustain life. They simply wanted to introduce themselves and let us know that the wonders of the universe might be closer than we ever imagined. And, get this," Nicholas grinned, "Dexter mentioned he'd like to give us a tour of their spacecraft—a journey that he assured us takes only 36 hours to reach Earth!"

Susan, initially skeptical, dismissed Nicholas's dream as mere fantasy, playfully reminding him that dreams rarely come true. However, a month later, their skepticism was shattered when, to their utter disbelief, a sleek, silver spacecraft materialized in their front yard, as effortlessly as a car pulling into a driveway.

Emerging from the craft were Dexter and Astral, looking every bit as magnificent as they did in Nicholas's dream. Their arrival sent shockwaves through the quiet neighborhood. Nicholas, still reeling from the unexpected turn of events, invited them in, his voice trembling with a mixture of disbelief and excitement.

"We would be honored to spend some time with you," Dexter replied, his voice a gentle baritone. "Perhaps four to five months, if that suits you?"

Overwhelmed by this extraordinary turn of events, Nicholas and Susan welcomed Dexter and Astral into their home as if they were a long-lost family. They were treated like royalty, given the warmest welcome imaginable, a privilege few could ever hope to experience.

As dust began to settle, painting the sky in hues of orange and purple, Dexter and Astral expressed their amazement at the Earth's twilight. "We have no such phenomenon on Mars," Astral remarked, her voice filled with wonder.

Nicholas and Susan, eager to make their guests feel at home, prepared a sumptuous dinner, a feast fit for royalty. They invited Dexter and Astral to freshen up while they finalized the preparations, eager to begin this extraordinary interplanetary exchange.

Dinner was a sumptuous affair, a feast for the senses. As they dined, conversation flowed easily between the four of them. Nicholas, unable to contain his curiosity, finally turned to Dexter. "You both are... well, breathtaking," he stammered. "How is it that the people of Mars are so... so incredibly beautiful?"

Dexter chuckled, a warm, melodic sound. "Ah, that, my friend, is a result of centuries of genetic evolution and a harmonious existence," he explained. "We strive for balance, not only in our physical well-being but also in our emotional and spiritual development."

He then proceeded to share insights about Martian society: "Mars, you see, is a planet of remarkable diversity, yet remarkable unity. A significant portion of our planet is meticulously maintained, a testament to our respect for nature. While there are regions that remain challenging to inhabit, much of our planet is a thriving ecosystem, much like your own Earth. Our population is approximately nine hundred million, with an average height of six feet five inches. We value peace and harmony above all else. Conflict is virtually nonexistent. Each family is limited to two children, ensuring a sustainable population. Our lifespan, thanks to advancements in medicine and a harmonious lifestyle, averages around two hundred years."

Dexter paused, a thoughtful expression on his face. "We have been aware of your existence for quite some time," he continued. "We have intercepted your radio transmissions, your attempts to reach out to the stars. We chose to observe you, to study your civilization, before making contact. We believe in peaceful coexistence and respect for all sentient life. Our journey here, though brief, is a gesture of goodwill, a first step toward a potential interplanetary dialogue."

He smiled gently. "We hope this encounter proves fruitful, Nicholas. Perhaps it's time to explore our own cosmic backyard before venturing further into the vast unknown."

Dexter continued his voice calm and measured, 'In our society, qualities like dishonesty, arrogance, violence, anger, and materialism are simply not tolerated. Honesty, compassion, and a deep respect for all life are the cornerstones of our existence. We find no need for religion, drawing our inspiration instead from the boundless energy of the sun and the interconnectedness of all living things.

'Our communication network is unparalleled. We can connect with anyone, anywhere on Mars, instantly. We have a visual network that allows us to see and interact with loved ones in real time, fostering a strong sense of community. And our transportation system is efficient and seamless, allowing us to travel anywhere on the planet with ease. Every two kilometers, you'll find community centers where people gather to discuss ideas, share knowledge, and simply enjoy each other's company.

'We understand that your world is still grappling with these concepts,' Dexter said gently. 'But we believe that a harmonious society, free from conflict and driven by a shared sense of purpose, is the key to a truly fulfilling existence.' He paused, a thoughtful expression on his face. 'We are here to learn from you as much as we hope to share with you. And believe me, we have plenty of time for that. Five months is but a blink of an eye in the grand scheme of things.'"

"Dexter continued, his gaze warm and thoughtful. 'We chose you, you see, because your dedication to exploring the universe resonated deeply with us. Your passion, your relentless pursuit of knowledge, it shone through in your research. We noticed your unwavering commitment, your willingness to dedicate your lives to unraveling the mysteries of the cosmos. And Susan,' he added, a gentle smile gracing his lips, 'we observed her unwavering support for your endeavors, even sacrificing her own career to join you on this incredible journey. Your love for each other, your shared passion for discovery, it was truly inspiring.'

He paused, then continued, 'We understand that the search for extraterrestrial life has proven challenging. NASA and other space agencies have been diligently searching for signs of life beyond Earth, yet the universe remains largely silent. But perhaps,' he suggested, 'the answers we seek are closer than we ever imagined.'

Dexter leaned forward, his eyes twinkling with amusement. "Now, it's your turn. Ask us anything. We are eager to answer your questions, to share our knowledge and experiences with you."

Astral, who didn't have to compliment Dexter as he had already provided good

background information, asked Susan if she had anything to ask before Nicholas.

Susan, still reeling from Dexter's revelations, found herself speechless for a moment. "I… I don't know where to begin,' she finally stammered. "It's all so… incredible."

Astral chuckled softly. "Would you like to visit Mars, Susan?" she asked. "With Nicholas, of course, and little Sally."

The question hung in the air, breathtaking in its simplicity. 'Visit... Mars?' Susan repeated, her mind reeling. "But... how?"

"Oh, travel between our planets is quite simple for us," Astral explained. "Our spacecraft can traverse the distance in a mere thirty-six hours. However," she added with a gentle but firm tone, "entry into Martian society is not granted for just anyone. We have a thorough screening process, a careful evaluation of an individual's character and values. We believe that the introduction of negative emotions—anger, greed, violence—would be detrimental to the harmony of our society."

She paused, her gaze turning towards Nicholas. "We understand that NASA and other space agencies are planning to establish colonies on Mars. While we welcome their efforts, we believe a careful selection process is crucial. The last thing we desire is for the delicate balance of our society to be disrupted by undesirable elements."

Astral's words hung heavy in the air, leaving Nicholas and Susan pondering the profound implications of this interplanetary encounter.

Nicholas, his curiosity piqued, turned to Dexter. "Could we... could we simply go with you in your spacecraft? Without any of that cumbersome space gear?"

Astral smiled. "Absolutely," she replied. "Our spacecraft maintains a comfortable Earth-like atmosphere. No need for any special suits or equipment during the journey."

Nicholas, his eyes widening, felt a surge of excitement. "And once we arrive on Mars?"

"You'll find an atmosphere very similar to your own," Dexter explained. "Oxygen-rich, breathable air, comfortable temperatures."

'However,' Astral added, 'entry into Martian society is carefully regulated. We have a thorough screening process for all visitors, ensuring the well-being of our society. Not everyone is welcome on Mars. We have conducted extensive scans of Earth, and unfortunately, we've identified three households in your immediate vicinity that would not be permitted entry. Their records indicate a history of criminal activity, and such behavior is simply not tolerated on Mars.'

Nicholas, startled, stammered, 'How… How did you scan Earth? I mean, your technology… it's incredible.'

Astral smiled gently. 'Our telescopes, Nicholas, are far more advanced than anything you've yet conceived. The James Webb, the Very Large Telescope – they are impressive instruments, but they merely scratch the surface. Our technology allows us to observe and analyze life on a much deeper level, to understand the very essence of an individual.'

The implications of Astral's words hung heavy in the air, leaving Nicholas and Susan speechless. The Martian visitors, with their advanced technology and seemingly utopian society, had just opened their eyes to a reality far beyond their wildest imaginations.

Dexter continued, 'On Mars, violence is simply not an option. We have no need for weapons of any kind. Guns, bombs, any form of aggression – they are simply inconceivable to us. In fact, we have a unique form of self-defense. Should anyone pose a threat, a simple gesture – a display of our palm, which contains a small, shimmering chip – is enough to neutralize the aggressor. It's a technology that ensures peace and harmony throughout our society.'

Nicholas and Susan exchanged a look, both deeply intrigued by this revelation.

'We would be honored to host you at our cottage on the nearby island,' Nicholas offered, eager to share a piece of his world with these extraordinary visitors.

Dexter and Astral graciously accepted the invitation. 'It would be a pleasure,' Astral replied.

The next morning, they set off toward the island, leaving their spacecraft parked discreetly in the driveway, its presence unnoticed by their neighbors. As they drove, Dexter remarked, 'Our roads on Mars are remarkably smooth, almost like gliding on air. We utilize a unique type of gravel, extracted from deep within our planet, combined with crushed volcanic rock. It creates a surface that is both durable and incredibly smooth.'

As they approached the waterfront, Dexter and Astral gasped in unison. The sight that unfolded before them—the shimmering lake, the lush green hillsides, the vibrant hues of the surrounding landscape—took their breath away. "This is… breathtaking," Astral murmured, her eyes wide with wonder. "The beauty of your planet is truly awe-inspiring."

Nicholas and Susan, touched by their genuine appreciation, smiled. Their island retreat, once a place of solace for them, was now about to become the stage for an extraordinary interplanetary exchange.

Dexter and Astral were overjoyed to be on the island. "This is truly idyllic," Astral remarked, her eyes sweeping over the lush greenery.

Susan, touched by their enthusiasm, offered to let Astral hold Sally. "She'd love to play with you," Susan smiled. Astral, with a gentle touch, took Sally into her arms. The little girl, seemingly sensing Astral's warmth and kindness, immediately smiled, reaching out to touch Astral's shimmering face.

Lunch was a simple yet elegant affair—grilled salmon with a medley of sautéed vegetables and a light teriyaki sauce. "Delicious!" Dexter exclaimed, his eyes widening. "The flavors are exquisite."

As they dined, they watched a nature documentary on television, focusing on the wonders of the universe, including a segment on Mars. However, the images shown were stark and desolate—barren landscapes, volcanic craters, and the remnants of old NASA rovers.

"Your technology," Dexter explained gently, "is still limited in its ability to truly capture the essence of Mars. Those images only show a small fraction of our world. The majority of Mars is lush and vibrant, with vast oceans, flowing rivers, and lush green forests. Your rovers, though impressive, have yet to explore the truly breathtaking regions of our planet."

They spent the next few days exploring the island, enjoying boat rides, fishing excursions, and evenings spent playing games and sharing stories. The Martian visitors, with their advanced technology, effortlessly mastered the human games, much to the amusement of their hosts.

Two weeks passed in a whirlwind of activity, filled with laughter, shared meals, and a growing sense of camaraderie between the two families.

Nicholas, eager to share his passion with his extraordinary guests, suggested, "Perhaps you'd be interested in visiting the Atacama Desert? We've been conducting research there, utilizing a very large telescope to observe the cosmos."

Astral, intrigued, replied, "We have indeed scanned that region of your planet. A fascinating area, rich in geological and astronomical wonders. However, I must confess, we would be delighted to experience it firsthand."

She turned to Dexter. "Perhaps we could take a brief excursion in our spacecraft? A quick tour of the desert, followed by a visit to the observatory. It should only take a couple of hours."

Nicholas and Susan, exhilarated by the prospect, readily agreed. Within moments, they were soaring above the desert landscape, the breathtaking vistas unfolding beneath them. The observatory, a marvel of human ingenuity, was a sight to behold.

Two weeks flew by in a whirlwind of activity. They enjoyed exploring the island, indulging in delicious meals, and sharing stories that spanned galaxies. Finally, the time for their departure arrived.

"It has been an unforgettable experience," Nicholas said, his voice filled with gratitude. "We will cherish these memories forever."

Dexter and Astral assured them that this was only the beginning of their friendship. "We invite you to visit us on Mars," Dexter said, "whenever you are ready. It will be our pleasure to welcome you to our home."

And so, two days later, with a mixture of excitement and apprehension, Nicholas, Susan, and little Sally embarked on an extraordinary journey, leaving the familiar confines of Earth behind and venturing into the unknown, towards a future filled with wonder and the promise of new beginnings.

The starship descended gracefully onto the Martian surface, its landing cushioned by a soft hum. Nicholas, Susan, and Sally, after a surprisingly comfortable journey, emerged feeling refreshed.

Astral greeted them with a warm smile. "Welcome to Mars," she said, her voice filled with gentle warmth.

Their home, a stunning structure of shimmering, translucent materials, stood majestically amidst a lush green lawn, reminiscent of Kentucky bluegrass. As they approached, a mechanism automatically removed their shoes, depositing them into a nearby vault.

Inside, a young man, his features strikingly like Dexter and Astral, greeted them with a tray of refreshing fruit juices and a platter of colorful vegetable fritters. "Welcome," he said, his voice a soft, melodic tone. "I am Kai, and I will be your host while you are here."

Little Sally, her eyes wide with wonder, eagerly reached for the fritters.

"Please, enjoy," Astral encouraged, her gaze filled with warmth. "We'll be right back. We just need to ensure your rooms are prepared to your liking."

As they settled onto the plush, bioluminescent sofa, Nicholas and Susan exchanged a look of awe. This was truly a world beyond their wildest imaginations.

Conversation flowed easily, a lively exchange of ideas and perspectives. As the evening wore on, little Sally grew tired, her eyelids drooping.

"Perhaps it's time for bed, sweetheart," Susan murmured, gently swaying Sally in her arms.

Nicholas pointed towards a shimmering, translucent elevator. "Or we could take the lift," he suggested. "It's quite a sight."

Intrigued, Sally giggled and reached out for the elevator buttons. The ride to their suite was a magical experience, the panoramic views of the Martian landscape unfolding before them. Their room was a masterpiece of design, a luxurious haven with technology seamlessly integrated into the environment.

After a relaxing evening and a refreshing night's sleep, they descended to the dining room, where Kai awaited them with a sumptuous breakfast. A colorful array of dishes adorned the table, including unfamiliar fruits that shimmered with an iridescent sheen. "These are called Solarian Berries," Kai explained, "a local delicacy."

CHAPTER 8

MARS, AS SEEN SO DIFFERENTLY.

After the meal, Dexter proposed, 'Why don't we take you on a tour of the township? We have a mode of transportation that might surprise you.'

Leading them outside, he gestured towards the spacecraft. 'This,' Dexter explained, 'can transform into a ground vehicle, capable of navigating any terrain.'

With a soft hum, the spacecraft began to morph, its aerodynamic form gradually transforming into a sleek, low-slung vehicle. Nicholas and Susan watched in awe as the transformation completed, revealing a luxurious, self-driving vehicle unlike anything they had ever seen before.

The vehicle glided smoothly along the streets, a gentle hum the only sound as they navigated through the meticulously planned township. Rows of elegant homes, no taller than two stories, lined the streets, creating a sense of tranquility and community.

'We believe in sustainable living,' Dexter explained, 'and prioritize harmony with nature. Hence the limit on building heights.'

Soon, they arrived at a circular plaza, a vibrant hub of activity. Ten towering structures, resembling futuristic obelisks, encircled the plaza. 'These are our community centers,' Dexter explained. 'Places where citizens gather to discuss local issues, share ideas, and contribute to the betterment of our society.

'We find that direct participation fosters a stronger sense of community and encourages active citizenship. It ensures that everyone has a voice in shaping the future of our society. And,' he added with a smile, 'since our society is largely free from conflict and scarcity, our discussions tend to focus on more... creative endeavors. Art, music, scientific exploration... the possibilities are endless.'

Nicholas and Susan were deeply impressed. This was a society unlike any they had ever encountered, a society where peace, harmony, and community were not just ideals but a lived reality.

Their exploration continued, and soon they arrived at an amusement park, a sprawling complex that reminded Nicholas and Susan of Disneyland. It was a welcome sight, a touch of familiarity in this alien yet captivating world.

Beyond the amusement park, a majestic mountain ridge stretched across the horizon, its slopes a vibrant emerald green. 'We're heading to meet some friends for lunch,' Astral explained. 'They're eager to meet our guests from Earth.'

As they approached their destination, a breathtaking vista unfolded before them. A luxurious restaurant, unlike anything Nicholas and Susan had ever seen, was nestled amidst a grove of shimmering trees. Each dining booth was a self-contained haven of privacy, with a personalized AI assistant, resembling Kai, available to cater to their every need.

A group of about twenty individuals, along with their families, awaited them. Introductions were made, and a flurry of curious glances and warm smiles were exchanged. Dexter and Astral, with a touch of pride, filled their friends in on every detail of their encounter with Nicholas and Susan.

'They are truly remarkable individuals,' Astral said, her voice filled with admiration. 'And their daughter, Sally... she's a delight.'

One of Astral's friends, a tall, elegant woman with eyes that shimmered like amethysts, turned to Nicholas and Susan. 'Would you perhaps be interested in joining us on a return trip to Earth sometime soon?' she inquired. 'We are eager to experience your world firsthand.'

Nicholas and Susan, overwhelmed by the unexpected invitation, exchanged a look. The prospect of sharing their world with these fascinating beings was both exhilarating and daunting.

'We would be honored,' Nicholas replied, his voice filled with a mixture of excitement and apprehension.

After the tour, they returned to Dexter and Astral's residence, their minds reeling from the sights and sounds of this extraordinary civilization.

'Life on Mars is truly remarkable,' Dexter observed, 'filled with wonder and a sense of purpose. There is no place for grief or sadness in our society. We strive for a life of joy and fulfillment.'

Nicholas, intrigued, inquired, 'How do you ensure such a harmonious existence?'

'Well,' Dexter explained, 'population control is crucial. We have a sustainable birth rate, ensuring that our resources are not overtaxed. And,' he added, 'we understand the importance of shaping young minds. A small, harmless chip, implanted at birth, helps to guide and nurture positive emotions and behaviors. It's a subtle influence, ensuring that aggression, anger, and negative emotions are minimized.'

Nicholas and Susan exchanged a thoughtful glance. 'On Earth,' Susan remarked, 'we struggle with these issues. Overpopulation, environmental degradation, conflict... it seems like humanity is constantly grappling with these challenges.'

Dexter nodded understandingly. 'We understand. Your world is still young, still learning. But I believe that humanity has the potential for greatness. You possess a unique spirit, a resilience that is truly inspiring.'

He continued, 'Our society is governed democratically, with elected administrators serving a twenty-five-year term. Their role is not to control but to guide and facilitate the ongoing evolution of our society.'

Nicholas and Susan listened intently, their minds grappling with the profound implications of Dexter and Astral's words. This was a society unlike any they had ever imagined, a society where technology was used not to control but to enhance the human experience.

Dexter continued, 'Our society has been observing the universe for millennia, much like yourselves. We've studied galaxies, black holes, stars, and exoplanets, searching for signs of other intelligent life. However, until now, we've only encountered life on two planets: Mars and Earth.'

He paused, his gaze turning towards Nicholas. 'We believe that our two civilizations can learn from each other. Together, we can address the pressing challenges facing humanity – war, poverty, and environmental destruction. Earth, despite its remarkable achievements, is currently on a perilous path. Uncontrolled greed, unchecked ambition, and a disregard for the well-being of our planet are leading us towards self-destruction.'

Dexter sighed. 'We observe the rampant growth of nationalism, the rise of extremism, the widening gap between the rich and the poor. Environmental degradation, the scourge of poverty, the constant threat of conflict… These are issues that plague your world. And while there are individuals and organizations striving for positive change, the overall trajectory seems… unsustainable.'

He continued, 'On Mars, we have learned to live in harmony with ourselves and with our planet. We have eliminated the root causes of conflict – anger, greed, and the desire for power. We have learned to value cooperation, compassion, and the well-being of all beings.'

Dexter extended a hand toward Nicholas. 'We offer our assistance, our technology, our wisdom. Together, we can help Earth achieve a sustainable future for all humanity.'

Nicholas and Susan were speechless, overwhelmed by the gravity of Dexter's words. The implications of his message were profound, challenging their own perceptions of humanity and the future of their world.

Nicholas, deeply moved by Dexter's words, replied, 'We are... we are truly humbled, Dexter. Overwhelmed, yes, but also incredibly grateful for this opportunity. For years, we have dedicated ourselves to exploring the cosmos, peering through telescopes, searching for signs of life beyond Earth. We never imagined that our quest would lead us here, to your remarkable world.'

He paused, reflecting on the profound implications of their encounter. 'The advancements we've made on Earth, in science, technology, medicine... They've been driven by a desire to improve the human condition. Yet, despite these advancements, we seem to be constantly on the brink of self-destruction.'

Susan added, 'War, poverty, environmental degradation... It feels like humanity is constantly fighting against itself. We are capable of such incredible things, yet we seem to be perpetually drawn towards conflict and destruction.'

Dexter nodded thoughtfully. 'We understand. Your world is still young, still learning to harness its full potential. But the potential for greatness is undeniable. It's time for us to work together, to share our knowledge and our wisdom. To ensure that the human spirit, this precious spark of life that emerged from the chaos of the cosmos, thrives and flourishes.'

He continued, 'We cannot allow fear, greed, or aggression to dictate our destiny. We must work together to create a future where peace, cooperation, and sustainability are not just ideals, but realities for all of humanity.'

Nicholas and Susan, deeply moved by Dexter's words, felt a renewed sense of hope. Perhaps, they thought, a brighter future for humanity was not just a dream, but a possibility, a reality that was within their reach.

Dexter suggested, 'As a starting point, we recommend you take with you a comprehensive collection of our documentaries. These cover a wide range of subjects – education, healthcare, social welfare, economic models, sustainable living, community building, and effective governance. We believe these resources, coupled with the guidance of your own government, can be invaluable in educating your populace about alternative approaches to societal challenges.'

He continued, 'Utilize your existing platforms, your social media networks, to disseminate this information freely and widely. Encourage open discussion, foster critical thinking, and empower your citizens to make informed choices. We believe that a well-informed and engaged citizenry is crucial for building a stronger, more just society.'

Dexter pointed towards the vibrant green spaces that lined the streets. 'Observe these walking and running paths. We constructed hundreds of them in every city, making physical activity accessible to all. But first, we educated the public about the importance of physical and mental well-being. We emphasized the link between physical activity and overall health, longevity, and happiness. Now, as you can see, these paths are teeming with people of all ages, enjoying the benefits of an active lifestyle.'

He paused, his gaze turning towards Nicholas and Susan. 'Your world possesses incredible potential. You have brilliant minds, groundbreaking technologies, and a spirit of innovation. However, you are also grappling with significant challenges – poverty, inequality, environmental degradation, and the threat of conflict. We believe that by sharing our knowledge and experiences, by collaborating on solutions to these global challenges, we can create a brighter future for all humanity.'

Nicholas and Susan were deeply moved by Dexter's words. They realized that the challenges facing humanity were not insurmountable. With cooperation, understanding, and a shared commitment to a better future, they could overcome these obstacles and build a world where peace, prosperity, and sustainability were not just dreams but a reality for all."

CHAPTER 9

INTERPLANETARY COOPERATION

"A month flew by in a whirlwind of activity. Nicholas and Susan, deeply impacted by their experiences on Mars, felt a growing sense of urgency. They knew they couldn't simply return to their old lives.

'We need to act on this,' Nicholas declared, his eyes filled with determination. 'We need to bring these ideas back to Earth and start making a difference.'

Dexter and Astral readily agreed. 'We are ready when you are,' Astral said. 'Let us return to Earth and begin this new chapter.'

Two days later, they boarded the spacecraft, their hearts filled with a mixture of excitement and apprehension. Joining them were Dexter and Astral, as well as two of their friends, a charming couple named Lyra and Orion, who were eager to experience Earth firsthand.

The journey back to Earth was swift and comfortable. Upon their return, they immediately sought out Nicholas and Susan's supervisor, Dr. Evelyn Walsh, a renowned astrophysicist.

Dr. Walsh, upon seeing Dexter and Astral, was speechless for a moment. 'This… this is truly extraordinary,' she finally stammered.

Dexter and Astral, with their characteristic grace, explained their mission and their desire to collaborate with Earth. Dr. Walsh, intrigued and excited by the prospect, readily agreed to join them on a return trip to Mars.

'This is just the beginning,' Dexter remarked, 'a first step towards a new era of interplanetary cooperation. We believe that together, we can overcome the challenges facing humanity and build a brighter future for all.'

Nicholas and Susan, watching the exchange unfold, felt a sense of profound hope. The future, once uncertain, now seemed filled with possibility. The dream of a united humanity, once a distant fantasy, was now within reach.

"Dexter suggested, 'As a starting point, we recommend you take with you a comprehensive collection of our educational materials – documentaries, simulations, and interactive experiences – that explore our societal values, our approach to governance, and our understanding of sustainable living. We believe these resources, coupled with the guidance of your own leaders and educators, can be invaluable in guiding humanity towards a more harmonious future.'

Nicholas and Susan exchanged a look, their minds racing with possibilities. This was not just a meeting between two civilizations; it was the dawn of a new era, an era of interplanetary cooperation and the potential for a truly transformative future for humanity.

'The first step,' Dexter continued, 'is to establish a dedicated Earth-Mars exchange program. We can facilitate the exchange of scholars, scientists, and artists, fostering cross-cultural understanding and collaboration. We can organize joint research projects, focusing on areas such as environmental sustainability, renewable energy, and advanced medicine.'

He paused; his gaze filled with a sense of purpose. 'The future of humanity depends on our ability to work together, to learn from each other, and to build a future where peace, prosperity, and sustainable living are not just ideals, but a reality for all.'

Nicholas and Susan, deeply moved by Dexter's words, felt a renewed sense of hope. The challenges facing humanity seemed less daunting now, a shared responsibility, a collective endeavor towards a brighter future.

The next few days were a whirlwind of activity. Dr. Walsh, a renowned astrophysicist and a woman of immense intellect and vision, immediately grasped the significance of this encounter. She recognized that this was not just a scientific breakthrough, but a turning point in human history.

Dr. Walsh, with the support of government officials and leading academics, began to implement a comprehensive plan for disseminating Martian knowledge and fostering interplanetary cooperation. The first step was a series of televised broadcasts featuring Dexter and Astral, where they shared insights into Martian society, their values, and their vision for a peaceful and sustainable future.

These broadcasts captivated the public imagination, sparking a global conversation about the future of humanity. People from all walks of life were eager to learn more about Mars, to understand the Martian perspective, and to contribute to the building of a better future.

The initial response was overwhelmingly positive. People began to engage in discussions about social issues, environmental concerns, and the importance of global cooperation. A sense of hope, a belief in a brighter future, began to permeate society.

This was just the beginning, a first tentative step on a long and challenging journey. But as Nicholas and Susan watched the global response unfold, they felt a renewed sense of optimism. The future, once uncertain, now seemed filled with possibility. The dream of a united humanity, a dream born on a small island on Earth, was finally beginning to take shape."

A new hope is taking shape in the general public's minds that an intelligent civilization is close by to Earth. The astrophysicists will continue observing and analyzing the stars and exoplanets in the vast universe, but at the same time, the governments on Earth would focus on the quality of life on Earth based on the Martian model. The joint research projects focusing on environmental sustainability, renewable energy, and advanced medicine became the main focus for collaboration between earth and Mars on an urgent basis. People from all walks of life suddenly started conversations about changing habits and adopting a progressive lifestyle like Martians. People started taking interest in the cosmic world. People at large started viewing our Earth as a cosmic entity and planet in light of a partner to other planets in this vast galaxy of ours. The dream of a united humanity, and the future, once uncertain, now seemed filled with possibility—a future where Earth and Mars, two civilizations once separated by the vastness of space, now could work together to create a better future for all.

Dr. Walsh, upon seeing Dexter and Astral, was speechless for a moment. 'This… this is truly extraordinary,' she finally stammered.

Dexter and Astral, with their characteristic grace, explained their mission and their desire to collaborate with Earth. Dr. Walsh, intrigued and excited by the prospect, readily agreed to join them on a return trip to Mars.

'This is not just a scientific breakthrough,' Dr. Walsh declared, her voice filled with a sense of wonder, 'but a turning point in human history. The Martian perspective, their emphasis on harmony, sustainability, and the interconnectedness of all life, offers a profound challenge to our current trajectory.'

The initial response from the global community was unprecedented. The televised broadcasts featuring Dexter and Astral captivated audiences worldwide, sparking a global conversation about the future of humanity. People from all walks of life were eager to learn more about Martian society, to understand their values, and to contribute to the building of a better future.

Social media platforms were abuzz with discussions about sustainability, environmental protection, and the importance of social justice. People began to question their own lifestyles, to re-evaluate their priorities, and to seek ways to contribute to a more just and equitable world.

Governments, inspired by the Martian model, began to implement policies focused on environmental sustainability, renewable energy, and social welfare. Education systems were revamped, emphasizing critical thinking, problem-solving, and global citizenship.

This was just the beginning, a first tentative step on a long and challenging journey. But as Nicholas and Susan watched the global response unfold, they felt a renewed sense of hope.

Now they had gotten the ball rolling, and the focus on interplanetary relationships was going to be stronger every day. The Earth was buzzing with Mars vibes and vice versa. Dexter, Astral, Lyra, and Orion created a new atmosphere in Earth's society and its physical beauty among the Martian community.

Nicholas and Susan, at the same time, focused on Sally's care. Sally was growing by the day. She was a joyful girl and had started schooling. She recalled her trip to Mars with her parents and talked about the trip to her classroom friends.

Dr. Evelyn Walsh was also expanding her field of operation in educating the populace on Earth globally. The success of this interchange between the two planets is yet to be seen sooner or later.

CHAPTER 10

TURN OF EVENTS

Nicholas and Susan planned a trip to attend a global summit of scientists, politicians, and social leaders, including the world's geophysicists. The summit was headed by Dr. Evelyn Walsh, and the main agenda was "The Martian Initiative"

The agenda was ambitious to promote and implement:

Sustainable development: Focus on renewable energy, resource conservation, and environmental protection;

Foster social equity: Address issues like poverty, inequality, and access to education and healthcare;

Cultivate global cooperation: Encourage international collaboration on issues such as climate change, disease prevention, and space exploration;

Promote peaceful coexistence: Foster understanding, tolerance, and respect among all cultures and nations.

The Martian Initiative, initially met with skepticism and resistance from some, gradually gained momentum. As the positive impacts of the Martian-inspired initiatives began to manifest – cleaner air, healthier communities, and a renewed sense of global cooperation – the world embraced the Martian vision with increasing enthusiasm.

Nicholas and Susan, observing these developments, felt a profound sense of satisfaction. Their encounter with the Martians had not only changed their own lives but had also set in motion a chain of events that would shape the future of humanity for generations to come.

Nicholas and Susan, exhausted but exhilarated, returned to their hotel room after the first day of the summit. 'What a remarkable day,' Susan exclaimed, pouring them both a glass of wine. 'The energy in that room… it was palpable.'

Nicholas nodded in agreement. 'The Martian perspective has truly shaken things up. They've challenged our assumptions, and forced us to confront the realities of our own world.'

They shared a quiet moment, their hands clasped together, reflecting on the profound implications of the day's events.

The following days were a whirlwind of activity. Panels were formed to address crucial issues: poverty eradication, environmental sustainability, education reform, and the development of a global framework for cooperation. It became clear that addressing poverty and inequality was paramount. As Dexter had pointed out, a truly just and equitable society could only be built upon a foundation of social and economic justice.

The summit culminated in a series of ambitious initiatives: a global fund for poverty alleviation, a massive investment in renewable energy, and a renewed commitment to environmental protection. Perhaps most importantly, the summit laid the groundwork for a comprehensive Earth-Mars exchange program, fostering collaboration in science, technology, education, and culture.

Years passed. Sally, now a bright-eyed young woman of 27, was pursuing her Ph.D. in astrophysics, following in her parents' footsteps. She often recounted her childhood memories of the Martian visitors, the awe-inspiring journey to Mars, and the profound impact those experiences had on her life.

One day, Dexter and Astral arrived on Earth for a visit, accompanied by their son, Drake. Drake, a remarkable young man with his father's striking features and his mother's ethereal grace, was a renowned architect specializing in the design of sustainable, eco-friendly structures, many of which incorporated unique Martian architectural principles.

Sally, now a prominent figure in the global sustainability movement along with her parents, was introduced to Drake. Both tall and elegant, they shared an instant connection. As they conversed, a sense of wonder filled the room. The future, once uncertain, now seemed filled with endless possibilities, a testament to the enduring power of interplanetary cooperation and the hope for a brighter future for all humanity.

Drake, and Sally went for a walk in a park near their home and discussed Martian life and life on Earth at length. Drake asked Sally if she would go with him to Mars on their return trip. She could stay there as long as she wanted and explore the Martian landscape. He would drop her back when she wished to be back to Earth. Sally gladly agreed to go with him to Mars. After a month, Dexter, Astral, and Drake took Nicholas, Susan, and Sally with them on their return trip to Mars. They wanted them to stay a little longer with them so that Sally can feel life on Mars. All of them arrived at their home on Mars. Sally was quite delighted to see their ultra-modern home. She was impressed with the design of the home made on Mars.

Dexter asked his son Drake if Sally wished to go with him sightseeing trip in the town. Sally heard this and shouted, "Yes, I would like to go sightseeing with Drake!" He asked their home helper, Kai, who was also driver, to take Drake, and their guest, Sally, for sightseeing trip in town. Kai prepared their convertible, and away they went. Sally was quite impressed with the town's beauty. She gasped, her eyes wide with wonder. Towering trees lined the streets, their leaves shimmering with an iridescent sheen. Buildings constructed from translucent materials seemed to blend seamlessly with the natural landscape. There were no signs of pollution, only clean air and the gentle hum of wind chimes. They stopped at a roadside complex where they had a Martian fruit drink, which was quite refreshing, as Sally had never tasted something like this before. Drake and Sally were looking at each other affectionately." This is incredible, "Sally exclaimed, taking a sip. I know, "Drake replied smiling. We have access to incredible fruits and vegetables here, grown in our hydroponic gardens. And the air is so pure and so clean." It's amazing, "Sally agreed. "I can see why you love it here." After a couple of hours of sightseeing, both were brought home as it was close to lunch hour.

During Sally and Drake's absence, Susan, Nicholas, Dexter, and Astral talked about Sally and Drake, saying Sally and Drake look perfectly fit for each other. Both parents agreed that they would make a unique couple. Astral mentioned that in Martian civilization, the mother of a son proposes to the daughter of a couple if she is willing to marry her son. This is done in front of both the families, friends, and relatives. Nicholas, and Susan already agreed to this. Astral had invited their friends and relatives for lunch at the community center. The center was a shimmering structure, where people hosted concerts, art exhibitions, and even interplanetary video calls with Earth. A hush fell over the gathering as Astral addressed Sally. 'Sally,' she began, her voice filled with warmth, 'we have observed you with great admiration. You are a bright, kind, and compassionate young woman. And Drake... well, he's always been a bit of a dreamer, but he's also a hard worker and a truly kind soul. We believe the two of you would make a wonderful pair,' She proposed to Sally if she would marry her son, Drake. Drake and Sally were delighted to hear this, and Sally quickly said yes.

A marriage ceremony was arranged, which was performed by one of the sun-worshiper friends in the community. An interplanetary marriage took place on Mars. The Martian friends and relatives of Dexter and Astral were amazed by this relationship and showered blessings on the bride and groom. Sally from Earth was a perfect fit for Drake on Mars. Both looked like a handsome couple, tall and graceful. The families' friends and relatives complemented Susan and Nicholas on this occasion. The guests brought bundles of gifts for Sally and Drake. Sally was surprised to receive the gifts, as she was thinking that the system of offering gifts looks simple and common on both planets.

"A month later, Sally, with a heart full of both excitement and trepidation, remained on Mars. Nicholas and Susan, their hearts heavy but filled with pride, returned to Earth aboard Dexter's spacecraft, piloted by the ever-capable Kai. Dexter and Astral stayed behind, overseeing the construction of a magnificent new home for Drake and Sally – a stunning structure of shimmering, translucent materials nestled amidst a grove of shimmering trees.

Dexter and Astral also oversaw the installation of a state-of-the-art observatory equipped with the most advanced telescopes imaginable, allowing for unprecedented observations of the universe, including a deeper understanding of those elusive eleven dimensions.

Sally, meanwhile, embraced Martian life with an enthusiasm that delighted everyone. She explored the vibrant cities, marveling at the innovative architecture, the lush green parks, and the harmonious coexistence of technology and nature. She learned about Martian culture, their history, their art, and their unique perspective on the universe.

One evening, as they enjoyed a leisurely stroll through a bioluminescent park, Drake, gazing at Sally with a mixture of admiration and affection, asked, 'Would you ever consider staying here, Sally? Forever, perhaps?'

Sally, her heart fluttering, replied, 'I've never felt more at peace, Drake. This place... it feels like home.'

As the years passed, Sally and Drake became renowned for their groundbreaking research in astrophysics, their discoveries pushing the boundaries of human understanding and paving the way for future interplanetary exploration. Their story, a testament to the power of love, hope, and interplanetary cooperation, became a legend, reminding generations to come of the extraordinary possibilities that arise when we embrace the unknown and strive for a brighter future for all."

CHAPTER 11

MORE MARS

Sally and Drake, while enjoying a leisurely stroll through a vibrant Martian park, began discussing the latest findings from the Perseverance Rover, which has made several significant discoveries, including:

Evidence of Ancient Lakebed: Perseverance found evidence of an ancient lakebed at "Wildcat Ridge," indicating that the area was once habitable for microbial life. This discovery further supports the idea that Mars may have once supported life.

Volcanic Rocks: The rover discovered igneous rocks, providing insights into the planet's volcanic history and the processes that shaped its surface.

Oxygen Production: The rover's MOXIE (Mars Oxygen In-Situ Resource Utilization Experiment) successfully produced oxygen from the Martian atmosphere, a crucial step toward future human exploration of Mars.

Sound Recordings: Perseverance recorded the sounds of the Martian environment, including the rover's own movements and the Martian wind, providing valuable insights into the planet's acoustic environment.

Collection of Rock and Soil Samples: Perseverance has collected and cached a diverse set of rock and soil samples, which are intended to be retrieved by a future mission and brought back to Earth for further analysis.

These findings have significantly advanced our understanding of Mars' past, present, and potential for future exploration and even human habitation.

Drake said, "I am willing to help in this area, and I am taking up the concern before our leaders to mobilize our resources to ensure that the entire Martian territory becomes habitable, and that we can open an immigration process for people from Earth". 'It's truly remarkable,' Sally replied, 'The potential for life, for a thriving civilization, right there on Mars.' They recognize that NASA has been actively exploring Mars and seeking evidence of past habitability and potential for future human settlements.

'Exactly,' Drake continued. 'But we need to remember that only a portion of Mars is currently habitable. The northern hemisphere, with its more temperate climate and potential for terraforming, offers the greatest promise. The southern hemisphere, with its harsh conditions and extreme temperatures, remains a significant challenge.'

'That's true,' Sally agreed. 'But with continued research and innovation, we can overcome those challenges. Imagine a future where the entire planet is transformed, where we can cultivate lush green landscapes, create sustainable cities, and expand the boundaries of human civilization beyond Earth.'

Drake smiled, his eyes sparkling with excitement. 'That's exactly what I envision. I believe we have a responsibility to explore these possibilities, to push the boundaries of human ingenuity. I'm determined to work with Martian and Earth scientists to develop sustainable terraforming techniques and create a future where Mars can truly become a second home for humanity.'

Sally, her heart swelling with pride, placed her hand on his arm. 'I'm with you, Drake,' she said, 'every step of the way.'"

They highlight the potential for a "second Earth": They emphasize that if Mars can be terraformed to become more Earth-like, it could become a viable home for a significant portion of Earth's population.

Drake expresses his commitment to this vision: He states his intention to advocate for increased efforts to make the entire Mars habitable and to support the development of an immigration process for humans to settle on the red planet.

Sally and Drake feel very enthusiastic. They hug and kiss each other passionately.

The next day both Sally and Drake discussed their future plans to make the entire Mars habitable with their parents and asked them to work with politicians, and scientists on both planets to achieve this goal as fast as possible.

Both Sally and Drake are excited to take their determination to the next level. NASA has been making incredible progress in understanding Mars, and they are eager to contribute their expertise in the same direction to see a thriving civilization, right here on Mars. They need to focus on making it a reality. Together, they can create a future where humanity thrives not just on one planet but on two. As they continued their stroll, hand in hand, they envisioned a future where the Southern part of Mars, once a desolate red planet, would bloom with life, a testament to the ingenuity and perseverance of the human spirit.

Drake mentioned to Sally that our planet Mars is known as the God of War on your planet, Earth. "Yes, I know. I read it and heard it through folklore," said Sally. "In fact, Mars has a rich history in mythology, often associated with war and strength due to its reddish appearance in the night sky. For example:

Roman Mythology: Mars was the god of war, a powerful and fierce deity. He was the father of Romulus and Remus, the founders of Rome, and was highly revered by the Roman people.

Greek Mythology: The Greek counterpart of Mars was Ares, also the god of war. However, Ares was often depicted as more brutal and chaotic than Mars.

Hindu Mythology: Mars is known as Mangala, the god of war and celibacy. He is associated with strength, courage, and aggression.

Chinese Mythology: Mars is called the "fire star" and is associated with the element of fire, representing passion, energy, and aggression.

In addition to these major mythological associations, some ancient cultures believed that Mars was inhabited by powerful spirits or gods, while others saw it as a harbinger of bad luck or misfortune.

Overall, Mars has played a significant role in human mythology and imagination, often serving as a symbol of war, strength, and power. Its reddish color and prominent position in the night sky have made it a source of fascination and wonder for people throughout the ages.

Mars' association with war stems from the planet's appearance in red color, caused by iron oxide on its surface, which is often seen as blood and fire, and both are linked to warfare in ancient cultures. Also, many early civilizations, including the Romans and Greeks, had deities associated with war in their pantheons. It's possible that the planet Mars, with its striking color, was a natural fit for these pre-existing ideas. In astrology, Mars is often associated with energy, action, and aggression. These traits can be linked to the god of war, further cementing the connection between the planet and the deity. Besides, Mars was also associated with agriculture and fertility. This aggressive feature of Mars has shaped the planet's name and its cultural significance for centuries.

With so much belief and myth about Mars, I am sure the planet must have had some elements of life on it, Sally added. Drake mentioned that we need to continue our efforts to plant life on the entire surface of Mars sooner or later.

CHAPTER 12

AGGRESSIVE EFFORTS

Currently, there is definitely a growing interest in the possibility of humans living on Mars! As we the reasons like,

Scientific curiosity: Mars is the most Earth-like planet in our solar system, and scientists are eager to learn more about its past, present, and potential for life.

Technological advancements: Recent advancements in space technology, like SpaceX's Starship, are making the idea of Mars colonization seem more feasible.

Human ambition: The drive to explore and expand beyond Earth is a fundamental part of human nature. Mars represents a new frontier and a chance to push the boundaries of what's possible.

Inspiration from science fiction: Mars has long captured the imagination of writers and filmmakers, fueling our fascination with the Red Planet and the possibility of life beyond Earth.

However, it's also important to acknowledge the challenges:

Harsh environment: Mars has a thin atmosphere, extreme temperatures, and no liquid water on the surface, making it a very hostile place for humans.

Technological hurdles: We still need to develop the technology to transport people and supplies to Mars, build habitats, and ensure long-term survival.

Ethical considerations: There are questions about the potential impact on any existing Martian life like yours with me, said Sally to

Drake hugging him tightly, the cost of such a mission, and who gets to go. Sally added that she is the lucky one to be with him because your parents visited our Earth.

Despite these challenges, the dream of living on Mars continues to inspire scientists, engineers, and space enthusiasts around the world. Whether it happens in our lifetime or not, the possibility of humans becoming a multi-planetary species is an exciting prospect that captures the imagination of many. The momentum towards Mars colonization is building, and it's an exciting space to watch in the coming years. While there is no guaranteed timeline, the convergence of private companies and government agencies working towards Mars habitation makes it a realistic possibility within the next few decades.

Sally said that Elon Musk's goal of establishing a self-sustaining Mars colony by 2050, with initial missions, and with your already developed technology and cooperation, is actively developing the Starship, which is reusable and transportable for humans and cargo, indicating that it may potentially happen much sooner.

Other private companies, such as Blue Origin, Virgin Galactic, and others, are also working on technologies for space travel and potential Martian habitation.

NASA is aiming to send humans to Mars in the 2030s and is developing technologies like the Space Launch System (SLS) and Orion spacecraft for this purpose. Other international agencies, like the European Space Agency (ESA), are also contributing to Mars exploration and potential habitation efforts.

Sally and Drake are very enthusiastic with already developing strategies taking place on Earth. They are quite hopeful and looking forward to seeing two Earths in this universe.

Susan turned to Drake, her eyes sparkling with excitement. "Can we swing over to the other side of Mars in your spacecraft, darling? I'd love to get a closer look at those canyons." She gestured toward the jagged, rust-colored landscape visible through the viewport of the *Ares VI*. The spacecraft, a marvel of engineering with its gleaming metallic hull and retractable solar panels, hummed gently as it orbited the planet.

Drake chuckled, a hint of amusement in his voice. "It's not going to work, love. *Ares VI* is designed for long-distance space travel, not maneuvering in a thin Martian atmosphere. We'd be lucky to get it off the ground, let alone fly it across the planet." He pointed to a complex schematic displayed on a nearby console. "We know that NASA and other agencies are working on terraforming, making the atmosphere more Earth-like, and *then* we'll be able to use something like this. You never know; maybe we'll get the latest model by then," he added with a wink. "In the meantime," he continued, his gaze returning to the Martian landscape, "we need to contribute our expertise toward solving the puzzle." A thoughtful expression settled on his face as he gazed out at the red planet.

Susan's shoulders slumped slightly. "Oh, that's a shame," she said, her voice tinged with disappointment. "I was really hoping to see those canyons up close." Then her eyes lit up. "But what about rovers? Could we use a rover to explore that area?"

Drake smiled. "That's a good idea, Susan. We do have a couple of rovers at our disposal. But the terrain over there is quite rugged, and it would take a long time to travel across the planet that way." He paused, his gaze drifting back to the viewscreen. "The puzzle," he said softly, "is understanding how life managed to evolve on Mars in such a harsh environment. If we can unlock that secret, it could revolutionize our understanding of the universe and even help us find life elsewhere."

Sally and Drake were invited to dinner by Drake's parents. The aroma of roasted vegetables and herbs filled the air as Drake and Sally entered Dexter and Astral's spacious home. Lyra and Orion, Dexter's friends and fellow scientists, were already seated at the dining table, engaged in a lively debate. Dexter, his brow furrowed with concentration, gestured toward a holographic projection of Mars hovering above the table. "The Martian leaders understand that a thicker atmosphere is crucial," he explained. "They're working on several fronts, from vaporizing the carbon dioxide ice at the poles to producing specific greenhouse gases like methane and water vapor."

"But methane is so potent," Lyra countered, her voice laced with concern. "Are we sure about the long-term effects? What about the potential for runaway global warming?"

Orion, ever the optimist, chimed in. "We have to take calculated risks, Lyra. The potential reward – making Mars habitable – is too great to ignore. Besides, we're developing sophisticated climate models to predict and mitigate any negative consequences."

Sally, whose research focused on Martian soil composition, perked up at the mention of perchlorates. "We've made some progress in identifying microbes that can break down perchlorates," she said, eager to share her findings. "Perhaps we can use bioremediation to transform the Martian soil into fertile land."

Drake, his eyes sparkling with anticipation, exchanged an excited glance with Sally. He was eager to contribute his expertise in atmospheric modeling to the project. "This is incredible," he said. "It's a challenge, no doubt, but imagine the possibilities..."

"I'm also studying the feasibility of constructing giant mirrors and lenses in space," Drake said, "to focus sunlight onto Mars and warm the planet. It's a massive undertaking, but the potential payoff is enormous."

"That's brilliant, Drake!" Lyra exclaimed, her eyes lighting up. "If we could effectively control the amount of sunlight reaching Mars, we could precisely regulate the temperature increase."

"And our scientists are also investing heavily in releasing trapped gases," Dexter added, pointing to a holographic map of Mars. "There's substantial evidence that Mars has vast reserves of carbon dioxide locked away in its polar ice caps and as carbonates in the soil. Releasing those gases could significantly thicken the atmosphere."

"But how do we control that release?" Orion asked, a hint of concern in his voice. "We don't want to trigger a runaway greenhouse effect."

Sally, whose expertise lay in Martian soil composition, chimed in. "And even if we manage to thicken the atmosphere and warm the planet, we still have the challenge of the perchlorates in the soil. We're making progress with bioremediation techniques, but it's a slow process."

"Terraforming the entire planet will be a project spanning centuries, perhaps even millennia," Sally continued. "It'll require immense resources, technological breakthroughs, and, most importantly, international cooperation on an unprecedented scale. In the meantime, these smaller-scale projects, like creating enclosed habitats and artificially warming small areas, are crucial. They're not just experiments; they're providing us with invaluable data that will guide our larger terraforming efforts in the future."

As they ate, the conversation continued, flowing easily between scientific details and more personal reflections on the implications of their work. The aroma of the herb-infused Martian vegetables filled the air, mingling with the excitement and anticipation that hung heavy in the room. Even with the daunting challenges ahead, there was a sense of optimism, a belief that humanity could, one day, make Mars a second home.

Drake and Sally were having breakfast when Drake's communicator chimed. It was a message from Dr. Evelyn Walsh. He tapped the screen to open the video call.

"Good morning, Drake, Sally," Dr. Walsh greeted them, her face beaming. "I have some exciting news. NASA is unveiling a prototype for a Martian habitat today! It's a modular design, using Martian soil and locally produced bricks for radiation shielding. The idea is to create round living quarters, almost like interconnected domes, that can be expanded as the colony grows. They're planning to house the first long-term Martian residents there to experiment with sustainable living practices."

A holographic image of the habitat model appeared on Drake's communicator screen. It was a striking structure, its rounded domes gleaming in the simulated Martian sunlight. "The walls are made of a composite material," Dr. Walsh explained, "combining Martian regolith with a binding agent. It's incredibly strong and provides excellent protection from radiation."

"That's fantastic, Evelyn!" Sally exclaimed, her eyes wide with excitement. "When will they begin construction?"

"They're hoping to start within the next Martian year," Dr. Walsh replied. "There's tremendous enthusiasm for this project, not just at NASA, but also in the political arena. Senator Ramirez has been a particularly vocal supporter, pushing for increased funding. And you wouldn't believe the number of people signing up for the Mars migration program! It's growing every day. They're undergoing rigorous training, both physical and psychological, preparing themselves for the challenges of living on another planet."

Drake, however, had a thoughtful expression. "That's all wonderful, Evelyn," he said. "But what about the long-term sustainability of the colony? Are we sure we can create a truly self-sufficient ecosystem on Mars?" He knew that even with the best planning, there were still many unknowns.

Dr. Walsh nodded. "That's a valid concern, Drake. We're working on that too. We're experimenting with closed-loop life support systems, developing ways to grow food using Martian soil, and exploring the potential for mining local resources. It's a huge undertaking, but we're making progress every day."

The video call crackled to life, Dr. Walsh's face filling the screen. "Sally, Drake, I have some exciting news!" she announced, her voice brimming with excitement. "The latest analysis from the orbital survey shows promising signs of subsurface water ice in the designated habitat zone. It's a much larger deposit than we initially estimated!"

Sally and Drake exchanged high-fives. "That's fantastic, Evelyn!" Sally exclaimed. "That water ice is crucial for our long-term sustainability. It'll provide drinking water, fuel, and even help us grow crops."

"And," Dr. Walsh continued, "the robotic construction teams have successfully assembled the first two habitat modules. They're using a new type of Martian regolith brick that's even more resistant to radiation than we anticipated." She displayed a 3D rendering of the habitat on the screen. It was a sleek, dome-shaped structure, partially buried in the Martian landscape for added protection.

"We've also made significant progress with the atmospheric modeling," Drake added, his voice filled with pride. "Our simulations show that the combined effect of the greenhouse gas injection and the release of trapped CO2 could raise the average Martian temperature by several degrees within the next decade."

"This is incredible progress," Dexter said, beaming. "It looks like our dream of establishing a permanent settlement on the other side of Mars might actually become a reality."

"But," Astral cautioned, "we still have so many challenges ahead. We need to develop reliable life support systems, find a way to make the Martian soil fertile, and, of course, address the ethical considerations of altering another planet's environment."

Despite the remaining challenges, a palpable sense of optimism filled the room. The teams on Mars and Earth were united by a shared goal: to make humanity a multi-planetary species. They knew the road ahead would be long and difficult, but the progress they had made so far fueled their determination to push forward.

CHAPTER 13

GROWING INTEREST TO IMMIGRATE

The newly opened Martian Immigration Office on Earth buzzed with activity. Hopeful migrants, clutching folders filled with documents, waited anxiously in line. A young woman named Anya, her eyes sparkling with excitement, chatted with a recruitment officer. "I've always dreamed of living on Mars," she said. "It's a new beginning, a chance to be part of something extraordinary."

Meanwhile, at the SpaceX facility in Texas, engineers huddled around a prototype spaceship, its sleek metallic hull gleaming under the bright lights. "Thirty-six hours to Mars," a technician muttered, shaking his head in disbelief. "It seemed impossible just a few years ago."

On Mars, in the newly established architectural offices, families browsed through catalogs of Martian home designs. Sally and Drake watched as a young couple, their faces filled with anticipation, selected a design for a small, two-dome dwelling. "It's not much," the husband said, "but it's a start. Our own little piece of Mars."

Outside the office window, the first experimental greenhouse shimmered under the artificial sunlight. Rows of leafy green vegetables thrived in the specially formulated Martian soil. Drake smiled. "We're making progress," he said to Sally. "It's slow, but we're getting there."

But later that evening, during a video conference with Earth, a note of concern crept into the conversation. "We've hit a snag with the spaceship production," an engineer reported. "There's a shortage of a critical component, and it could delay our launch schedule."

The news cast a shadow over the optimism of the day. The dream of a thriving Martian colony was still within reach, but the challenges were far from over.

"It's time to start thinking about sending people," Sally said, tapping her pen against her desk. "Right now, we're just processing documents, keeping a record of applicants. We need to have a solid number for that first batch of settlers."

Drake nodded, his brow furrowed in concentration. "I agree. And I'm working on a plan to ramp up spaceship production. Nothing moves without a reliable fleet." He grabbed his jacket. "I'm heading over to the assembly plant now. Want to come?"

At the spaceship plant, the air buzzed with the hum of machinery and the clang of metal. Drake walked along the assembly line, inspecting the nearly finished spacecraft. He stopped to talk to the plant manager. "How are the component supplies looking?" he asked.

"Under control, Mr. Drake," the manager replied. "We've secured contracts with multiple suppliers to avoid any bottlenecks."

Back on Earth, in the bustling immigration office, an officer sat across from a young couple, their faces filled with hope. "We're so excited!" the woman said. "We were wondering, could we put in an application for our cousin too? He's always dreamed of living on Mars."

The officer smiled politely, but her expression was firm. "I understand your enthusiasm," she said, "but the rules are very clear. Each application can only include one dwelling. We're trying to ensure a fair and organized process for everyone."

"But our cousin could join us a few months later, right?" the man asked. "We could build another dome next door."

The officer sighed. "I'm afraid I can't guarantee that. Future applications will be considered based on available resources and colony capacity. We want to avoid any irregularities and ensure that the initial settlement runs smoothly. The rules on Mars are quite stringent, and we need to adhere to them from the start." She handed them a brochure outlining the immigration guidelines. "Please review this carefully," she said. "It explains the process in detail." The couple's faces fell slightly, but they nodded in understanding.

Six months after the paperwork was finalized, ten spacecraft, gleaming silver against the blue backdrop of Earth, pierced the atmosphere and began their journey to Mars. Each craft carried ten hopeful settlers, the first wave of humanity's expansion beyond Earth. Thirty-six hours later, the first craft touched down on Martian soil, followed by the others at twenty-minute intervals.

Tanya, her face pressed against the viewport, gasped. A wave of disbelief washed over her. "It's real," she whispered, tears welling up in her eyes. Through the dust-streaked window, the red hills of Mars stretched out before her, a stark and breathtaking landscape. And in the distance, a kilometer away from the landing pad, a row of gleaming domes shimmered under the Martian daylight. The dwellings, constructed from large, reddish-brown regolith bricks, looked like a futuristic village nestled in the Martian terrain.

As the spacecraft's ramp extended, Tanya took a deep breath and stepped onto Martian soil. The air was thin and cold, but the excitement coursing through her veins warmed her from the inside out. The landing pad was a hive of activity, ground crews in brightly colored suits directing the newly arrived settlers. A row of solar-powered lights illuminated the pathway to the dwellings, and Tanya could see patches of green – Martian plantations – flourishing in designated areas. Even the water fountains, surrounded by the solar lighting poles, looked strangely beautiful in this alien landscape.

Tanya joined the other settlers as they made their way to their assigned homes. Her dwelling was small but cozy, with a panoramic window offering a stunning view of the Martian landscape. As she settled in, a sense of awe washed over her. This was it. She was on Mars. Humanity had finally established its first foothold on another planet. It was a monumental achievement, a testament to human ingenuity and the enduring spirit of exploration. The mission, against all odds, had been accomplished.

CHAPTER 14

THE EARTH ATMOSPHERE ON MARS

High above Mars, a colossal structure of mirrors and lenses, painstakingly assembled over years, reflected the sun's rays onto the red planet. Inside the control center on Earth, Drake watched the temperature readings climb steadily. "It's working!" he exclaimed, a triumphant grin spreading across his face. "The temperature is rising faster than our most optimistic models predicted!" His team erupted in cheers, years of research and dedication culminating in this moment.

On Mars, Sally and her team carefully monitored the bioremediation process. "The perchlorates are breaking down!" she announced, her voice filled with excitement. "The microbial agents are working even better than we hoped. We can start planting the test crops soon." Nearby, a robotic arm extended from a greenhouse, carefully placing a seedling into the treated Martian soil.

Deep beneath the Martian surface, powerful drills bored through the ice, unearthing vast reserves of frozen water. "We've struck a major vein!" a geologist reported to the surface team. "This should be enough to supply the colony for years to come."

Inside the Martian habitat, the first settlers were adjusting to their new lives. They wore specialized suits when venturing outside, but inside the domes, they could breathe the artificially generated air, a mix of nitrogen and oxygen produced by plants like the experimental MOXIE unit. They tended to the burgeoning crops in the greenhouse, their faces filled with hope as they watched the first Martian vegetables sprout from the soil.

The scientists, both on Earth and Mars, knew that this was just the beginning. They were already planning the next phase of terraforming: introducing more complex plant life, creating a more sustainable ecosystem, and continuing the long, arduous process of making Mars a true second Earth. The challenges were still immense, but the initial successes had ignited a fire of optimism. Humanity's dream of a thriving Martian colony was slowly but surely becoming a reality.

The invitation came during a video call. Nicholas's face filled the screen, his eyes twinkling. "We were wondering," he began, "if you and Kamla would like to join us on Mars. We'd love for you to see our home there."

Susan chimed in, smiling warmly. "Sally and Drake have agreed to take you on their next starship. It would be wonderful to have you both."

My heart skipped a beat. Mars! It was a dream I'd harbored for years, a fascination with the red planet that had started in childhood. "Are you serious?" I asked, hardly daring to believe it.

"Absolutely!" Nicholas replied. "We know how much you've always wanted to go. And Kamla's been talking about seeing the Martian landscape for ages."

I glanced at Kamla, who was listening intently. Her eyes mirrored my own excitement. "We'd be honored," I said, my voice filled with emotion. "Thank you, Nicholas, Susan."

"It's our pleasure," Susan said. "We'll coordinate with Sally and Drake and let you know the details soon."

The call ended, and Kamla and I exchanged excited glances. "Mars!" she exclaimed, a wide smile spreading across her face. "I can't believe it's actually happening."

"Me neither," I said, still a little in shock. "It's like a dream come true."

True to their word, the details came quickly. A few weeks later, a message arrived from Sally and Drake, confirming our trip. We were scheduled to depart in three months. The reality of our Martian adventure was sinking in, and the anticipation was almost unbearable.

Kamla and I began the preparations, but the phrase "packing" felt inadequate. This wasn't a two-week resort holiday; this was Mars. We consulted the official Martian Colonist Handbook, a thick binder filled with regulations and recommendations. It listed everything from specialized clothing for the thin atmosphere and fluctuating temperatures to personal hygiene items designed for low-gravity conditions. "This is more like preparing for an expedition," Kamla said, chuckling as she sorted through a pile of thermal underwear.

I was equally overwhelmed. My suitcase, usually reserved for business trips, now held a collection of freeze-dried meals, radiation-shielding accessories, and a first-aid kit that looked more like a miniature medical clinic. I also packed a few sentimental items – photos of family, a favorite book, and a small, hand-carved wooden bird that my grandfather had made. It felt important to bring a piece of Earth with me to this alien world. This gear is important if needed.

When I spoke with Drake and Sally again, I couldn't contain my enthusiasm. "We're almost ready!" I exclaimed. "Just a few more things to pack, and we'll be good to go. Kamla's already practicing her low-gravity walk," I added with a laugh.

"That's great!" Sally replied, smiling. "We're so excited to have you both. We've got a few things to finalize on our end, but we'll send you the final itinerary next week. Get ready for an adventure of a lifetime!"

The thought of setting foot on Mars, of seeing the red landscape with my own eyes, filled me with a sense of wonder. It was a journey into the unknown, a step into the future. And I couldn't wait.

Off we go to Mars:

Can't wait to be on Mars

The journeys will continue

AUTHOR BIO

Nityanand Sharma is a retired Education Superintendent with a passion for reading and writing. He enjoys a wide range of genres, including romance, fiction, and adventure. His own life story as an immigrant is captured in his autobiography, "My India My Canada: Finding My Place Between Two Cultures," published by Friesen Press in 2017. Nityanand arrived in Canada on September 9, 1968, after earning a Masters Degree in Economics and Public Administration from the University of Rajasthan, Jaipur, India. He was awarded a scholarship by Brandon University to complete an Education 1 Diploma, which led to a career teaching in secondary schools in Manitoba. During his career in education, he also earned a Pre-Master's Degree in Education Administration.

REFERENCES

Explora.com:

Atacama Desert: "Physical Geography of South America" (Oxford University Press

-Scientific Journal: "Journal of Arid Environments"
-Eso.org: For European Southern Observatory (ESO) and Paranal Residencia:
-The Antofagasta: Official Tourism Websites:
-NASA Official Website: nasa.gov: